Madison stepped away from Luke.

Since their one unforgettable night together, Luke was constantly on Maddie's mind.

When she was close to him, any semblance of her lawyerly deductive reasoning flew right out the window. And when they were in the same room, she felt a physical ache to be in his arms.

Maybe if she had never known the magic of letting him possess her…

And here she'd thought that finally losing her virginity would simplify her life. Ha!

She still wasn't certain why she'd let Luke—client, confirmed bachelor and longtime buddy—be the first.

But if things could get more complicated, she wasn't sure how.…

Dear Reader,

The year is off to a wonderful start in Silhouette Romance, and we've got some of our best stories yet for you right here.

Our tremendously successful ROYALLY WED series continues with *The Blacksheep Prince's Bride* by Martha Shields. Our intrepid heroine—a lady-in-waiting for Princess Isabel—will do anything to help rescue the king. Even marry the single dad turned prince! And Judy Christenberry returns to Romance with *Newborn Daddy*. Poor Ryan didn't know what he was missing, until he looked through the nursery window....

Also this month, Teresa Southwick concludes her much-loved series about the Marchetti family in *The Last Marchetti Bachelor*. And popular author Elizabeth August gives us *Slade's Secret Son*. Lisa hadn't planned to tell Slade about their child. But with her life in danger, there's only one man to turn to....

Carla Cassidy's tale of love and adventure is *Lost in His Arms*, while new-to-the-Romance-line Vivienne Wallington proves she's anything but a beginning writer in this powerful story of a man *Claiming His Bride*.

Be sure to come back next month for Valerie Parv's ROYALLY WED title as well as new stories by Sandra Steffen and Myrna Mackenzie. And Patricia Thayer will begin a brand-new series, THE TEXAS BROTHERHOOD.

Happy reading!

Mary-Theresa Hussey

Mary-Theresa Hussey
Senior Editor

Please address questions and book requests to:
Silhouette Reader Service
U.S.: 3010 Walden Ave., P.O. Box 1325, Buffalo, NY 14269
Canadian: P.O. Box 609, Fort Erie, Ont. L2A 5X3

The Last Marchetti Bachelor

TERESA SOUTHWICK

SILHOUETTE *Romance*

Published by Silhouette Books

America's Publisher of Contemporary Romance

For Karen Taylor Richman and Joan Marlow Golan.
Thanks for encouraging me to take a chance.
I hope you're as pleased with the results as I am.

SILHOUETTE BOOKS

ISBN 0-373-19513-3

THE LAST MARCHETTI BACHELOR

Copyright © 2001 by Teresa Ann Southwick

This edition published by arrangement with Harlequin Books S.A.

® and TM are trademarks of Harlequin Books S.A., used under license.
Trademarks indicated with ® are registered in the United States Patent
and Trademark Office, the Canadian Trade Marks Office and in other
countries.

Visit Silhouette at www.eHarlequin.com

Printed in U.S.A.

Books by Teresa Southwick

Silhouette Romance

Wedding Rings and Baby Things #1209
The Bachelor's Baby #1233
*A Vow, a Ring, a Baby Swing #1349
The Way to a Cowboy's Heart #1383
*And Then He Kissed Me #1405
*With a Little T.L.C. #1421
The Acquired Bride #1474
*Secret Ingredient: Love #1495
*The Last Marchetti Bachelor #1513

*The Marchetti Family

Silhouette Books

The Fortunes of Texas
Shotgun Vows

TERESA SOUTHWICK

is a native Californian who has recently moved to Texas. Living with her husband of twenty-five years and two handsome sons, she is surrounded by heroes. Reading has been her passion since she was a girl. She couldn't be more delighted that her dream of writing full-time has come true. Her favorite things include: holding a baby, the fragrance of jasmine, walks on the beach, the patter of rain on the roof and, above all, happy endings.

Teresa also writes historical romance novels under the same name.

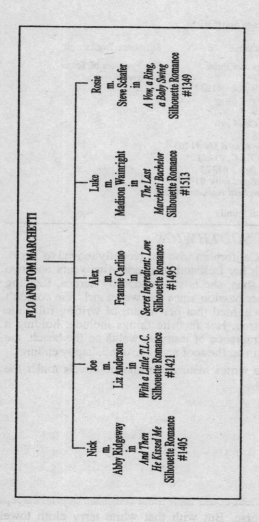

FLO AND TOM MARCHETTI

Nick
m.
Abby Ridgeway
in
*And Then
He Kissed Me*
Silhouette Romance
#1405

Joe
m.
Liz Anderson
in
With a Little T.L.C.
Silhouette Romance
#1421

Alex
m.
Frannie Carlino
in
Secret Ingredient: Love
Silhouette Romance
#1495

Luke
m.
Madison Wainright
in
*The Last
Marchetti Bachelor*
Silhouette Romance
#1513

Rosie
m.
Steve Schafer
in
*A Vow, a Ring,
a Baby Swing*
Silhouette Romance
#1349

Chapter One

"**I** understand leaving without telling me goodbye." Luke Marchetti's deep, accusing tone said he didn't understand at all. "But I don't get why you didn't tell me you were a virgin."

Madison Wainright froze in her bedroom doorway and took a deep breath.

Turning to face him she whispered, "Luke."

"In the flesh."

And what exceptional flesh he had. He stood beside her queen-size four-poster bed, his thick dark hair still damp from his shower. His smoldering bad-boy good looks took her breath away—the well-shaped nose, square jaw shadowed with whiskers, and dormant dimples. When he scowled, like now, they were barely there. But she'd seen him flash a smile, unleashing dimples that looked as if a sculptor had pressed thumbs into soft clay. The effect could melt most feminine hearts. Except hers, of course. But with that white terry cloth towel loosely knotted and slung low on his lean hips, he could be the poster boy for tall, dark, dangerous and tempting.

"Why, Maddie?"

While he'd showered, she'd debated whether or not she could face him after doing "the deed." Finally she'd slipped on jeans and a T-shirt. Now she pressed a cardigan against her breasts, as if that could shield her from his gaze. Since he'd already seen her without a stitch, it was rather like closing the barn door after the horse got loose.

"Why am I leaving my own condo? Or why didn't I tell you about the 'V' issue?"

"Either. Both." He lifted his powerful shoulders in a shrug.

He was her three-dimensional definition of the word *hunk,* not that she'd had gobs of personal experience evaluating the opposite sex in various stages of undress. But she was nothing if not opinionated. And her opinion was that she liked his tall, lean body. She liked the hair on his chest.

Stubbornly she resisted the urge to sigh. Even now she remembered the way her right palm had tingled as she'd run her hand across the oh-so-masculine contours. Now, in the daylight, she added visual to her tactile memory and saw that the dusting of hair tapered to a vee just above the spot where his pesky plain white towel tenaciously clung as if by magic to his hips.

He looked out of place in her frilly, feminine surroundings: lace curtains covered the windows; vases filled with flowers adorned the dresser and nightstand; wreaths and bows and pictures of Victorian women hung on the walls; even the bed, covered in white eyelet, shouted that this was a woman's world. The sight of floral sheets, twisted and tangled from loving Luke the night before, flooded her with guilt.

She was no longer Southern California's last twenty-five-year-old virgin. But, why, why, why had she let it be Luke?

She swallowed twice before regaining the power of speech. "I realize this is my place. As a thoughtful hostess concerned about your privacy, I figured it would be better if I slipped out quietly." She tried for an impersonal, businesslike tone, so the breathless quality in her voice was a dismal failure. "Just call me Martha Stewart," she added, struggling for lightness.

Ignoring her humor, he asked, "Better for who?"

His manner was almost friendly and conversational, but his blue eyes narrowed at the same time as his full, sensual lips thinned. She knew she would never forget the feel of his mouth on several of her most super-sensitive spots.

"Better for both of us—to spare us the awkward morning-after-the-night-before dialogue."

"Sharing the experience afterward is the best part. But you wouldn't know about that, since it was your first time."

"Are you making fun of me?"

"Never. I'm annoyed that you neglected to tell me." He crossed his arms over his chest.

The defensive pose limited her view. But her disappointment was mitigated by the impressive muscles that bunched in his biceps.

"Okay. Busted. You're right. I've never done this before. On top of that, I don't read women's magazines. I don't know the top ten topics of discussion the morning after spending the night with a man for the first time. Or the politically correct behavior. My experience is in the courtroom, not the bedroom. I don't like feeling inept. There are things I can do to get ready for court, but there's no way to prepare for—what we did last night. I was just trying to spare both of us an uncomfortable situation. I'm sorry I was such a disappointment.''

His nostrils flared slightly, as if he was a beast in the wild scenting his mate—again. ''I never said I was disappointed. Just the opposite.''

She met his gaze, and her breath caught at the primitive look in his eyes. Electric-blue, she thought. What does that mean? Probably that she would get zapped. Again. Which was exactly why she'd wanted to slip out quietly, even though this was her place.

He took a deep breath and let it out slowly, making his mouth seem even more exciting, if possible, than last night. She already knew that one touch of his lips to hers made her other four senses stand at attention, anxiously anticipating their turn.

Somehow, she had to sever the sensuous spell surrounding her. She studied his face and said the first thing that came to mind. ''You didn't shave.''

''I don't have a razor. And a good thing, too. If I'd taken the time, you'd have escaped.''

Still in the doorway, with freedom so near, she clutched her sweater tighter. ''Escape. Right. I do have work to do.''

She sounded like a moron but hoped he wouldn't notice. Or that he would be noble and just let her off the hook.

''What's your rush? It's Sunday. Even a workaholic like you is off today. If nothing else, city hall has the good sense to close the courts on the weekend.''

Apparently, he wasn't feeling especially noble this morning. ''True. But most of a lawyer's work is done before setting foot in the courtroom. Besides I have groceries to buy, and—''

''Hold it, Maddie.''

Maddie. He was the only one who ever called her that. It had been her undoing last night. She'd always been Madison. Her mother had insisted on it. She'd picked up the habit of correcting anyone who tried to shorten her name. Why had she never admonished Luke?

''What?'' she asked.

''Ever since Nick, you vowed never to get involved with another Marchetti man. I know for a fact that you've never been with another man. I have to know— why me?''

He was right about her vow. She'd made it just over a year ago, after her relationship with his brother Nick hadn't worked out. His heart belonged to another woman. That didn't come as a big surprise. She wasn't the sort of woman men fell for. Growing up the way she had tended to do that to a girl. The split with his brother had been amicable, and Luke had offered her a shoulder to lean on. Which she had refused. Even though his shoulder was just one of many parts to admire in such a fine specimen of a man.

Her career had to be her focus. She didn't want an intimate relationship. Although it would be a humdinger of a challenge to have a relationship *less* intimate than she had shared with Luke last night. So what in God's name had possessed her to sleep with him? Because he swept her away? He had, but it was so not like her to lose control.

She just didn't have any answers. ''Objection. The question is irrelevant.''

''It's relevant to me.'' He sighed heavily. ''You're twenty-five. You're a beautiful, green-eyed redhead.''

"You should get your eyes checked." She pointed to her nose. "These freckles are hateful little suckers and pretty unattractive."

"I like them. I imagine a lot of guys like them. In fact, I bet guys hit on you all the time. So why now and why me?"

"I wish I knew."

If only she could chalk up her weakness and temporary suspension of brain function to too much liquor at his brother's wedding the night before. But she'd only had the one glass of champagne Luke had fetched for her to toast Alex and Frannie, and she hadn't finished that. Luke had been attentive from the moment she'd arrived at the elder Marchetti's home without a date for the wedding. Her law firm represented the legal interests of Marchetti's Incorporated. Since she'd become a friend of the family, she was the representative chosen to attend. Alone. Luke had been alone, too, which she didn't understand since he was a babe magnet.

He'd just said guys must hit on her all the time, and she could say, "Right back at you." A man who looked like him had to give the general female population whiplash when he walked into a room. Yet in all the time she'd known him, he'd never settled on one woman. Why in the world would she be foolish enough to believe she could be the one?

But she'd been grateful for his presence beside her at the fairy-tale June wedding. For some reason, as the festivities had wound down, she'd been oddly reluctant to return to her lonely town house. He'd taken her for a drive. When it came out in conversation that he'd never seen her place, she'd invited him over. One thing had led to another. But he deserved a more articulate answer to his question about why him.

"I'm not sure why, Luke," she started. "Motive and opportunity."

He flashed a grin and treated her to the world-class dimples that made her knees weak. "Spoken like an up and coming attorney."

Cursing the fact that she hadn't made a quicker exit, she met his intense, blue-eyed gaze. "That's right. I'm a lawyer on the fast track. I was handpicked by Jim Mallery to take over his clients when he retired. Virgin, high-powered attorney is an oxymoron. Sort of." She shrugged.

"That doesn't answer my question. Why me?"

"That's the opportunity part."

His lips thinned for a split second. "I was hoping for something less premeditated. Something more along the lines of that you lost your head and couldn't help yourself."

She hoped he would never know that he'd just hit the nail on the head. But losing her head was a half step from taking a blowtorch to her heart. Burned once she was naive; burned again she was just stupid. Nick fell for someone else because he realized she, Madison, wasn't love material. She wouldn't make the mistake of letting herself be vulnerable again.

"I would have appreciated advance warning that it was your first time," he said.

"Why? What difference would it have made for you to know that I'm a vir—" Heat started in her neck and radiated upward into her cheeks. "I mean that I *was* a virgin."

He pushed away from the bedpost and walked toward her. He stopped at a point where another of his long strides would put him a whisper away from her. A delicious fluttering started in her abdomen.

"It makes a big difference," he said, an angry edge to his voice. "Number one, I might have backed off. Number two, it's a big responsibility."

"Why?"

The word popped out of her mouth before she could stop it. Followed quickly by mortification. Curiosity had put her in the top 3 percent of her law school class. Now she just felt socially backward and pretty much humiliated.

"A woman's first time has an impact on every subsequent encounter. There are things a guy can do to make it easier—to make it good."

"It *was* good," she blurted out.

The slow half smile that turned up the corners of his mouth excited her at the same time it made her nervous. Had she just given him some sort of secret to use against her?

"I'm glad," he said. Then he frowned. "I don't buy the opportunity part of your explanation. This is me," he said, tapping the chest she'd so recently admired. "I know guys must come on to you all the time. You still haven't explained why me."

She sighed. "I'll answer that as best I can, Luke, but I'm not sure I know myself. I was caught up in the magic of the wedding." She smiled, and couldn't help that it was sad around the edges. "It was wonderful to be a part of a big happy family again."

"You're still hung up on Nick?" His voice was just this side of a growl. "Did it bother you hearing their announcement about Abby's pregnancy?"

"I was never hung up on Nick." There was no point in elaborating. He didn't need to know that guys figured out fast that she wasn't lovable. "I realized that it wasn't him as much as your family I missed. I never had that, a large, loving family,'' she said wistfully.

Or one that loved her at all.

"I thought you had a brother."

"I do. Older. But we're not close. Not with my parents, either."

"So you were raised by wolves?"

She laughed. "Just the thought would give my mother the vapors. No. Boarding schools, accelerated classes, a law degree. Oh, my," she said, struggling for humor as a defense against the assault of lonely, painful childhood memories.

"I think there's more to it than that."

Uh-oh. This was exactly what she'd been trying to avoid. "Don't, Luke."

"Don't what?"

"See things that aren't there. I'm not looking to get involved."

"With me?"

"With any man. But the last Marchetti bachelor tops the list."

"I'm not looking to get involved, either."

"Good," she said, popping that tiny bubble of disappointment before it even got started. "Why not?" she asked before she could stop herself. Her penchant for blurting out questions was her greatest strength and weakness.

He lifted one muscular shoulder in a casual shrug. "I figure after all this time of it not happening, it's just not in the cards for me. But there's no reason why we can't be friends."

After what we did last night? she wanted to shout at him. But she kept her cool and said, "I don't want to waste your time."

"Shouldn't I get to decide if it's a waste? It's my time."

"Which would be squandered on me. I'm offering you a painless out."

"You think love hurts?"

"Exactly," she said. Mostly she meant loving and not having it returned.

He shook his head, and she hated the pitying look he leveled at her. "I'm not sure I buy your explanation."

She shrugged. "Every crime has motive and opportunity."

"And you think what we did was a crime?"

"Maybe more like a misdemeanor. But certainly not very smart. Don't you agree?"

"Not by a long shot." His eyes narrowed. "I don't buy this act of yours. You're not a swinging-singles woman. In spite of your profession, you're not a manipulator. You're not a calculating person. I think for the first time maybe in a long time, you let yourself feel. We were good together, Maddie. We like each other. You got caught up in the moment. You already admitted it was good. From a woman's first time, there's nowhere to go but up."

Oops. She had given him a weapon to use against her. "It can't happen again, Luke."

"It could," he said. He raised one dark eyebrow in a suggestive expression that easily kicked up her heart rate. "If you'd let it."

"I won't. Even if I wanted to, which I don't," she hastily added, hoping he wouldn't suspect that she'd just lied. "Your family is one of Addison, Abernathy and Cooke's oldest and most influential clients."

"But you dated Nick."

"That was before I was handpicked to handle your

company's legal business. Now there's a huge potential for conflict of interest.''

"There's no conflict. I'm definitely interested.''

"Be serious, Luke.''

"I've never been more serious. I don't see how us being friends would be a problem.''

"Because you're not a lawyer. At the very least, a close personal association with a client suggests the appearance of impropriety. And even if I believed in love, it would be unprofessional of me to continue seeing you. I'm nothing if not professional.''

His gaze raked her from head to toe. "In jeans and T-shirt you look about eighteen. But denim on you in court would sway judge, jury and opposing male counsel to whatever you were selling.''

"You're not helping,'' she said, blushing furiously.

"Good. I hope I'm making it hard as hell for you to dismiss me.''

"I'm not dismissing you. But all we can achieve is a friendly working relationship.''

"We achieved way more than that. And we can't go back, Maddie.''

Yes, she could. And there was no time like the present. "The name is Madison.''

"Since when?''

"Since we woke up in bed together.''

Four weeks after Maddie—correction Madison—had shut him down, Luke sat in his office trying to focus on the spreadsheet program staring at him from his computer screen.

It was almost quitting time, but his bachelor condo held little appeal. And his thoughts kept straying to a petite, green-eyed redhead, her shoulder-length hair curly and wild after he'd run his hands through it.

He leaned back in his leather chair, linking his fingers before resting his hands on his abdomen. He was CFO of Marchetti's Incorporated. The family restaurant business was thriving, and he had a million things to do. But even the word *spreadsheet* brought visions of him and Maddie tangling her bedsheets into his mind, in direct competition with his concentration. Four weeks, for God's sake. She'd made it clear that they had no chance. Why couldn't he get her off his mind?

He was over thirty. He'd known lots of women. He'd done more than his share of dating and a good percentage of those dates had ended up with him spending the night. But he'd easily forgotten them. Why not Maddie? And, dammit, she would never be Madison to him. Frustration curled and knotted in his belly. Did a redhead's legendary temper spill over into stubbornness? Because she'd picked a hell of a time to display it. What was wrong with having a friendship? He knew better than to ask for forever after.

He got the feeling that her hesitation to get involved went deeper than she'd told him. He supposed it could have something to do with him, with the fact that he was the black sheep of the family. The only one with blue eyes, more keep-to-himself than outgoing, and the only one just under six feet tall. Except for his sister, Rosie. The point was, he was different. He figured he'd caught a recessive gene *not* to fall in love; therefore, home, hearth, family wasn't in the cards for him.

So why should Maddie take a chance on a guy like that? Especially after her relationship with his brother had fizzled?

Still, Luke would bet his Marchetti's Incorporated

stock options that Maddie had been telling the truth about not being heartbroken. After discovering she was a virgin, he was even more convinced. Or was that just wishful thinking?

The intercom on his desk buzzed, startling him from his thoughts. He leaned over and punched the button. "Yes?"

"Miss Wainright to see you," his secretary said. "And I'm leaving for the day."

Just the sound of her name booted up his pulse. "Send her in," he answered, trying to keep the hot-damn-I-can't-believe-she's-here tone out of his voice. "Have a nice evening, Cathy."

"Thank you," she answered before clicking off.

Maybe Maddie had changed her mind and they could achieve more than a friendly working relationship. What other reason could she have for coming to his office? Glancing at his computer monitor, he was reminded that she had been handpicked by a senior partner to handle his family's legal affairs. There could be a dozen things other than his scintillating personality and animal magnetism that had brought her here. She was unpredictable; the night spent in his arms was proof of that.

He'd best not count on anything with the enigmatic Ms. Wainright. Until notified to the contrary, he would assume she'd come to see him about business concerning Marchetti's Incorporated. The more business they did together, the sooner he would be able to get her out of his mind. That's the way it always worked for him.

His office door opened, and the counselor in question walked in. "Hello, Luke."

"Hi." He stood up. His father had drilled it into all four of the Marchetti boys to stand when a lady entered the room.

"Do you have a minute?" she asked.

"Of course. Take a seat," he said holding out a hand to indicate the leather wing chairs in front of his desk.

He'd rolled up the sleeves of his white dress shirt to just below his elbows first thing that morning and loosened his tie. He resisted the urge to straighten it and button his cuffs. With Maddie, he'd experienced an unforgettable, intimate night. He was a loner, not charming like his brothers. He'd learned *forever* wasn't in the cards for him. But he couldn't shut the door on the present, either. No way were the barriers going back up between them. At least on his part.

In fact, he figured it couldn't hurt to remind her. "To what do I owe the pleasure of a visit from the golden girl of Addison, Abernathy and Cooke?"

The color in her cheeks deepened to a becoming rose, and he knew his barb had produced the desired result. Her blush highlighted her soft skin and the freckles dotting her nose. He liked the way she couldn't quite hide them with makeup. There were exactly six. He knew because he'd kissed every last one.

She was still standing halfway between the closed door and his desk. Her hesitation to come closer and to answer him put a bump in his ego road, slowing it down. In fact he became uneasy. Usually direct, forthright and no-nonsense—the fact of her virginity being the only exception—this was a Maddie he'd never seen before. Her restrained behavior was unusual. Not to mention the worry puckering her forehead.

"It's nice to see you, Maddie."

She flinched. "I asked you to call me Madison."

"I remember." He'd always been good with figures, but hers was his favorite. He recalled every curve, every square inch of silky, sweet-smelling skin in spite of the tailored green suit she wore with the jacket buttoned to her neck. "So what brings you here? Business or pleasure?"

"It's personal, Luke."

Was she finally beginning to see things his way? She wasn't exactly wearing the expression of a woman looking to pick up where they'd left off. In fact, she looked pale, and tired.

"What is it, Maddie? Are you okay? You look like someone died."

"Someone did."

His chest felt tight and he had trouble drawing in air. The names of his loved ones flashed through his mind. Ma, Dad, Nick, Joe, Alex, Rosie, their spouses, his niece and nephew. Then common sense asserted itself. If something had happened to one of them, Maddie wouldn't be standing in front of him with the news. Come to think of it, as long as his family was fine, he couldn't see that he had much of an emotional investment in the person she was here to discuss. In fact, he'd go it one better. Whoever had died couldn't directly affect him, so whatever had brought her here after four long weeks was a lucky break for him.

He took a deep breath. "Okay. I'll bite. Who died?"

She swallowed once, then walked toward him. Finally she sat down in one of the chairs facing his desk and set her briefcase on the floor beside her. "I don't know how to tell you this."

"Just spit it out. Who died?"

She swallowed twice, then looked him straight in the eye. "Your father. Not Tom Marchetti," she added quickly.

"Since I'm not adopted, I haven't a clue what you're talking about."

"There's no easy way to say this. Tom Marchetti is not your biological father, Luke. The man who is— was—your father passed away."

Chapter Two

"**Y**ou're joking," Luke said.

She flinched a little at the politely disbelieving expression on his face. "I wish I were."

"This isn't funny, Maddie."

She didn't have the heart to bust him for using the nickname. Although she would never admit it, she liked it when he called her that. "I know. Believe me, I'm as shocked as you are."

"Who said I was shocked? Except about the fact that you would lie."

She let out a long breath and shook her head, kicking herself for the umpteenth time because she'd let her libido loose and allowed it to run away with her. A random act of passion was like a pebble tossed into a pond, rippling outward and touching so much more than that one tiny spot. She just hadn't realized that it was a really big pond or exactly how far those ripples could touch.

"Do the words *conflict of interest* ring a bell? This is

the reason it's not a good idea for an attorney to sleep with her client," she snapped.

The words were out before she'd thought them through. How she wished she could call them back, because the last thing she wanted to bring up for discussion was that night, the most unforgettable hours of her life.

"I don't see what one has to do with the other," he said.

"Then I'll explain it to you. If our association hadn't taken a personal turn, you would have no reason to mistrust me or question my behavior, or accuse me of lying."

"Sure I would. You're telling me that Tom Marchetti is not my father. That my mother slept with another man and I'm the result. My parents have been happily married for thirty-five years. This is the most preposterous thing I've ever heard. It has to be a lie."

"Come on, Luke. Think for a minute. This would be a stupid thing to fabricate. It's too easy to find out the truth. Besides, this is my work. It's my livelihood and my life. I take that very seriously. It's my fiduciary responsibility to handle this client's last will and testament. That's what I'm doing."

"Okay," he said. "I'll assume for a minute that you're telling the truth. Which means you've known about this. Do the words *lie of omission* mean anything to you? At the very least, I thought we were friends. But you never said a word to me about this."

"Number one, if I *had* drawn up the will, I would have been bound by client confidentiality not to reveal the terms. Number two, I inherited this file when Jim Mallery retired. He recommended that I take over his clients, including this one. But I didn't know anything about this until the firm received the news about Brad Stephenson's death.''

"That's his name?"

"Your father's?" she asked.

"My father is Tom Marchetti." His mouth tightened into a stubborn, angry line.

"In every way that counts—yes, he is your father. But not biologically."

"Give it up, Maddie. This is ridiculous. And even if it wasn't, why should I believe you?"

"The will Brad Stephenson had drawn up and on file with my firm is proof,'' she answered.

"Let me see it,'' he demanded, holding out his hand. Madison noticed that his fingers shook. "I didn't bring it with me. I'm here as your friend as well as an attorney. When you've had a chance to absorb what I've told you, we'll discuss the terms at the office. And we *are* friends, in spite of what you may think. That's why I'm here in person. News this sensitive couldn't be delivered over the phone.''

She saw several emotions cross his face and named every one: anger, disbelief, shock, betrayal and back to disbelief. This news would take time to assimilate. More passionate ripples on the proverbial pond. Her heart ached for him, and she wished she could put her arms around him and just hold him. But attorneys dealt in facts, not feelings. And she needed to keep this professional, not personal.

He speared her with a skeptical look. "So the only proof you can give me is your word that some wacko, who retained the services of an attorney from your firm, left something to me in his will. Does that about sum it up?"

"I would alter some of your wording slightly, but in essence your assessment is correct."

"You know, if you were upset about what happened between us, Maddie, all you had to do was say so."

She took a deep breath and folded her arms over her abdomen. "It's been a month, Luke." Please don't let him read anything into the fact that she knew exactly how long it had been. "If I was upset, don't you think you would know before this?"

"I'm not sure what you would do," he answered. "Creating such an elaborate fabrication—"

"I understand that this is a shock, Luke," she said, interrupting. She'd developed a thick skin over the years, trying not to let things hurt. Like the fact that her parents didn't want her. That she would never be enough to make them love her. But it hurt her a lot that Luke could believe for even a moment that she would make up a lie this hurtful to get even for something. His low opinion was like a physical blow, and she had no idea why it should matter so much to her.

She met his gaze squarely. "Taking it out on me won't get you anywhere." She reached into her suit jacket for the business card she'd put there. Leaning forward, she set it on his desk. "That's the number for one of the firm's associates. When you're ready, give him a call, and he'll advise you in this matter."

"What about you?" he asked.

She shook her head slightly. "I'll plead workload as an excuse to bow out. It's the most discreet way to handle the situation. No one has to know about us."

"What if I still want you?" His question was almost a growl, but the sensual undertone made her shiver.

She still wanted him.

She looked into his eyes, wondering if she was reading her own need and longing into his expression, his words, even though there was an edge to his voice that she'd never heard.

"The fact that you could even entertain the notion I'm lying indicates that you don't have confidence in me. You can trust Nathan McDonald completely," she said, lifting her chin to indicate the card she'd given him. Why had she thought he knew her at all? If he did, he wouldn't have accused her of something so slimy. "Nathan is the firm's expert in this sort of thing. I'll fill him in on the pertinent information and let him familiarize himself with the contents of the will. I'll let him know you'll be in touch."

Touch. The word evoked images of his hands gliding over her skin, raising tingles in their wake. Countless times since that magical night the memories had taunted her. Just one of her many punishments for breaking a cardinal rule. She blinked the seductive vision away.

"What makes you think I'll call?" he asked.

"Because you're not the kind of man who will let this slide. You're going to want answers. And they'll have to come from your mother. When you get them, you'll call," she finished, nodding confidently. She curled her fingers around the handles of her briefcase and started to stand.

"Ma is going to be pretty upset about these accusations—" He stopped when she gripped the arms of the chair and lowered herself into it again. "Are you all right?"

She nodded. "A little dizzy. I forgot to eat lunch. Give me a minute, and I'll leave you alone."

He stood up. "You look white as a sheet. Are you sure you're okay?" His brow furrowed with worry as he rounded his desk and stopped in front of her. "Maybe I should drive you somewhere,'' he said, putting his warm palm to her forehead.

The touch felt wonderful. A glow started in her abdomen and quickly spread north and south. He was worried about her. No one worried about her. Her mother had made it clear she'd been an inconvenient accident. Her parents were always too much into their own lives and grooming her older brother to take over the family business to concern themselves with her. And if a problem arose, boarding school personnel did their job just enough to avoid liability.

But she knew Luke's concern was offered instinctively—good news and bad. It meant that he was a kind and decent man.

But he was also a client, one who had avoided marriage for this long. That fact spoke volumes. It seemed clear to her that he didn't want the responsibility of worrying about *any* woman on a permanent basis. And her parents hadn't wanted her, why would anyone else? No, she didn't want anything personal or permanent, either. There was too much potential for pain. Which was the main reason she'd shut the door on anything between them, after she'd given in to temptation and spent those hours in his arms. She had learned to count only on herself; she was committed to advancing her career.

Their one night of passion had destroyed the chance of any relationship between them, either friendship or business. When she'd brought him this unbelievable news, his first thought was that she'd lied. She understood that he was reeling from what she'd told him, but she couldn't help being hurt that he could entertain the idea of her stooping so low, even for a moment.

What would he say if he knew there was more? Would he believe her? She didn't have the words, the heart, the courage to tell him what she suspected. Not now. But she would tell him. When she had confirmation.

"Maddie?" he asked. "You zoned out. Are you sure you're all right? Maybe I should take you home."

"No, thanks."

The last time he'd done that was what had gotten her into this conflict of interest in the first place. Now she was the least of his concerns. When he talked to his mother, and she knew he would, the facts would come out, because Flo Marchetti was an honest person, one of the finest women Madison had ever known. Studying the law had taught her that there were always mitigating circumstances. In spite of the way this looked, she hoped Luke would open his mind to those circumstances in order to find understanding and forgiveness.

He had a lot on his plate. It was best for both of them if they made a clean break from each other right now. He was going to have a lot to deal with. She wouldn't add another problem to the pile.

She smiled. "I'm fine. Just low blood sugar. I carry protein bars in my purse for this very thing." When the dizziness passed, she stood and backed away, putting a safe distance between them. "I'm sorry about all of this, Luke. You probably don't believe that, but it's the truth. If there's anything—"

"There isn't," he said too quickly. "If you're sure you're all right, I'll say goodbye, Maddie. I have work to do."

She walked to the door and stopped. "While you're working, do me a favor," she said, with her hand on the knob.

"What's that?"

"Remember that no one's perfect. We all make mistakes."

She stepped out and closed the door behind her, leaning against it with a sigh.

"Mistake is my middle name," she said to herself.

"Ma, you're not going to believe the whopper Maddie Wainright told me a little while ago," Luke said.

He walked into his parents' house, and the kitchen door wasn't even closed before the words were out of his mouth.

Flo Marchetti grinned at him fondly. "You know, ever since you were a little boy, you've always blurted out whatever was on your mind."

Luke studied her. With the newspaper spread out before her, she was sitting at the oak table set in the breakfast nook. It was as if he was seeing this kitchen and her for the first time. The ceramic tile countertops were the same. The tile floor hadn't changed, and neither had the side-by-side refrigerator that always held enough food to feed an army. Which was almost what the five Marchetti kids were.

Rewind that last part. If Maddie was telling the truth, there were only four Marchetti kids and one... His gut clenched. The pain was right there, scratching at his consciousness. He refused to feel it. Surely there was a mistake. When he figured it all out, he could let the pain go without allowing it to touch him. He released a long breath as he looked at his mother.

In her late fifties, she was still an attractive woman. Gray hair, cut stylishly short, framed her relatively unlined face. She was wearing an olive-green, two-piece, knit lounging outfit. Granny glasses perched on the end of her nose for reading. Above the lenses, affection seemed to reach out to him from her warm-brown eyes just the way it always had. But everything felt different. He was looking at the world through different eyes. Why had he never questioned the fact that his were blue? Neither of his parents or any of his siblings had eyes that color. Had he suspected something and just ignored it?

There was still the possibility Maddie was trying to punish him, although he didn't see her as that kind of woman. Maybe she felt guilty about spending the night with him. No one knew about it, but maybe she still wanted to make him pay. But she was right when she'd said if she was going to lie, the matter of his paternity would be too easy to prove.

"It's not a whopper," Flo said, pulling his attention back to her. "Maddie loves you."

"That's not the whopper, and she's never said that to me." Just the opposite. She hadn't said it in so many words, but when she'd left his office, he knew it was for good. Part of him rebelled at the thought. But he couldn't think about that now.

He met his mother's gaze. "Ma, when are you going to get it through your head that love doesn't make the world go round?"

"Never. Because it may not make the world go round but it sure makes the journey a lot more fun."

"Maddie handles my legal affairs. That's all."

"Even though you spent the night together after Alex's wedding?"

"How did you know— I mean—"

"Her car was parked here overnight because you drove her home."

Good grief, he felt like a randy teenager caught sneaking out of the house in the dead of night to meet a girl.

That wasn't far from the truth. Even though she had come to him with this preposterous story, he felt the need to protect Maddie.

"That doesn't mean that I stayed with her."

"Did you?"

Instead of responding directly he said, "You didn't say anything to anyone else, did you?"

"I didn't have to. Nick and Abby came by the next day for brunch. They were the ones who told your father and me." There was a self-satisfied expression on her face. "I always could tell when you were lying."

Had he inherited that trait? Would he be able to tell if she was lying? His head pounded as doubts reared up again. They had glided and swirled through his mind as he'd driven straight from his office at Marchetti's Incorporated to this house where he'd grown up. What if Maddie hadn't been lying? What if Tom Marchetti wasn't his father? That would mean his mother had slept with another man. No. It couldn't be true. Again pain threatened and he pushed it away.

"Where's Dad?" he said, nearly choking on the word. It wasn't the question he wanted to ask. He wasn't sure he was ready to hear the answer.

"Your father is having dinner with Rosie, Nick, Joe and Alex. You know he refuses to give up the tradition he started before you and your sister were born of giving me a night off by taking all his children out for dinner." She frowned. "Come to think of it, why are you here and not with them?"

"I forgot. I had a lot on my mind." He recalled the dinners with his Dad and siblings. They had done it once a week when they were all younger. Now the get-togethers were less frequent because of their busy schedules. But they made an effort to meet once a month at one of the Marchetti restaurants.

"Have you eaten, dear?" She started to stand. "I can make you something. Sit down."

Ignoring her invitation, he asked, "What did you do while Dad took us out?"

Flo looked thoughtful. "Usually I had a long, relaxing soak in the tub. I didn't have to play referee or listen to little fists pounding on the door. It was heaven for a frazzled young mother. Your father, bless his heart, realized that with three small boys a year apart in age, I needed some time for myself." She smiled. "So tell me about Madison and the whopper."

"She came to my office today," he started, watching his mother's face.

"That's a start. Togetherness breeds familiarity—or something like that," she said with a laugh. "I've always thought the two of you—"

"Ma, there is no two of us—"

"Have you ever heard the expression 'One is a lonely number'? It's about time you got yourself a love life. You're not getting any younger, Luke. You work too hard. Soul mates don't grow on trees. You've got to get out there and shake some branches. Find Ms. Right. Maddie is a wonderful girl—"

"I didn't come here to discuss my love life."

"Then why did you come, dear?" she asked calmly. "I can tell you've got something on your mind. What's troubling you?"

"Your love life."

She laughed. "Very funny. Every time your father or I have made allusions to our love life you kids make gagging noises and clear the room."

His nerves cranked up a notch. He had to know about her love life. "Do you know a guy named Brad Stephenson?" He gripped the back of the wooden chair until his knuckles ached.

Her body language was all the answer he needed. She went completely still as her eyes widened and her skin paled. "Brad Stephenson?" she whispered.

"So you do know him." Blood pounded in his ears. The barrier between him and the threatening pain cracked.

She nodded. "He was your father's accountant years ago."

There could still be a misunderstanding. Just because she knew him didn't mean she'd slept with the man. "Maddie came to the office today and you won't believe the wild story she told me. This guy Stephenson died—"

"Oh, no," his mother gasped as her hand fluttered over her breast.

"You cared about him?" he asked, studying her shocked expression. The knot in his gut tightened a notch.

"Tom and I both liked him," she said cautiously. "I'm sorry to hear he's passed away."

"Here's where the whopper comes in." He swallowed hard to get the words past the constriction in his throat. "He left a will, and Maddie inherited the account. She says I'm the beneficiary, that the guy is my father. Can you believe that?"

Flo sighed as she took off her reading glasses and set them on the table. She closed the newspaper and folded it in half, then quarters. The moment stretched into what felt like an eternity as his mother gathered her composure.

Lifting a gaze filled with tragedy, she said, "It's true, Luke. Brad Stephenson is your father."

Stunned didn't begin to describe what he felt. He could hardly breathe. It was as if hands had reached into his chest, squeezing all the vital organs he needed to draw in a single breath of air. It was as if her words tapped into a motherlode of shock. Pain flooded him. He couldn't get his mind around the fact that his mother, his Rock of Gibraltar on all things, could have done what she was saying.

"It was a long time ago," she continued. "I'd like to explain—"

"And about damn time, don't you think? When were you going to tell *me*?" Hurt and betrayal made him go cold inside.

She stood up and looked him straight in the eye. "Don't take that tone with me. I'm still your mother and deserving of your respect."

"Does Dad know? I mean Tom. Does he know?"

"Of course he does. I wouldn't keep something like that from him."

"But you kept it from me."

"You were a baby."

"I'm not now." He stared at her. "Does anyone else know?"

"Your brother Joe."

"Half brother," he clarified.

She lifted her chin slightly. "I had to tell him. He was having a personal crisis. I talked to him so he could work some things through. He needed to understand that every relationship goes through ups and downs. What doesn't kill you makes you stronger. I also gave him permission to tell all of you about it. Apparently he decided not to. He doesn't know about you, just my indiscretion—"

"Such a tidy word for it," he said. "Isn't there a neat little word for what I am?"

"Don't talk like that."

"Why? I believe the correct term is bastard. Or maybe the fact that you were married at the time makes it less ugly. Or more ugly? Maddie's right. I'll have to call her office and get legal counsel just to find out what label to use."

He was behaving like an idiot. But he couldn't seem to help himself. She'd *lied* to him about something as basic as who he was.

"Stop it, Luke. Let me explain—"

"You just did. But here's the abbreviated version. You slept with another man while you were married to Dad—sorry. Tom. It's going to take some time to get the principal players and labels straight."

She held her head high. "Even condemned criminals get an opportunity to defend themselves. If you'll just give me a chance—"

"I'm thirty years old. Seems like you've had plenty of chances." He ran a hand through his hair. "Neither you or Tom felt the need to explain to me that I'm living a lie." It wasn't a question.

"Because you're not. Your father and I had problems in our marriage. We worked them out. We both love you very much. Never doubt that—"

"Don't have doubts? That's asking an awful lot. You've let me grow up in a fantasy. Hell of a way to get a reality check, by the way. From the family attorney. Give me one good reason why I should believe you now?"

She laced her fingers together, and he was struck by her dignity in the face of his angry tirade. As soon as the thought entered his mind, he pushed it away. She'd cheated. She'd lied. How could he admire anything about her?

She drew in a deep breath. "Whatever ugly names you're not calling me to my face are no less than I deserve. But know this, Son—"

"Don't call me that," he ground out.

"I will," she said firmly. "You are my child, my son. I love you unconditionally. There's nothing you could do that would make me stop loving you. I did as any mother would—what was best for you. Your father and I discussed—"

"Which father? Sorry, but you're going to have to be more specific. I hit the jackpot today. Count 'em." He held up two fingers. "Not one but two dads."

She flinched, but ignored his sarcasm, and went on in the same modulated tone. "The adults concerned discussed the situation and felt you would be better off raised in a secure environment with a family who loves you."

"I fail to see how lies translate into love," he retorted.

"I hope you'll come to understand why we made the decision. In time, when you're less bitter and angry, maybe you'll see that we had your best interests at heart." She shook her head. "I don't understand. Brad promised. He agreed it was best not to say anything—"

"But he did." Pain and anger knotted together in his gut. "And in a whacked-out sort of way, that's some comfort. At least he had a conscience. Maybe I got his gene for telling the truth instead of yours to perpetuate a lie."

"Luke, listen—"

He turned away and walked toward the door. He heard her footsteps behind him. She put a hand on his arm and he couldn't break her hold without more force than he was willing to use. Meeting her gaze, he put his hand on the knob.

"Luke, you can be as angry as you want at me. But don't you dare take this out on your father. And don't pretend you don't know who I mean. Tom Marchetti loves you—you *are* his son."

"When you bury your head in the sand, you leave your rear end exposed," he shot back.

She went on as if he hadn't spoken. "I will not tolerate any disrespect toward your father."

As much as he hated to admit she was right about anything, the truth was Tom Marchetti was a victim, too. He wasn't the one who had slept with someone else.

"Don't—" Whatever she saw on his face made her release his arm.

Without a word from her to stop him, he left the house. He walked across the back grass, skirted the pool area ringed with Malibu lights, and stopped beside his sports car parked in the alley.

The anger, pain, bewilderment and betrayal that had dogged him since Maddie broke the news cascaded over him in a tidal wave that threatened to drown him. How could he have not known his whole life was a fabrication? The woman who had taught him right from wrong, who had given him a moral foundation to live by, had lied to him in the most elemental way. How could he not be bitter and furious?

Happy childhood memories washed over him. Times spent with his siblings, his mother—the man he'd never had a reason to question as his father. How could they let him grow up believing he was a part of that? As a teen, he'd been grounded from his car for trying to pull a fast one. Yet she expected him to act as if nothing had changed for him. How hypocritical was that? *Everything* had changed.

Leaning against the driver's door, he ran both hands through his hair. His mother had given him the answers, just as Maddie had said. And she was right. He definitely planned to call a lawyer. But a stranger couldn't respond to the questions he had. In fact, there was one big one at the top of his list, one that overshadowed everything else.

"Who the hell am I?" he whispered into the dark night.

Chapter Three

A week after breaking the news to Luke, Madison stared at the blinking cursor on her office computer screen and silently begged it to spit out just the right words. He had taken her advice, made an appointment and would be there any minute. She had to hand him over to her associate. And she had to tell him she was going to have a baby. She'd done the test—several times, different brands. Pink and plus signs danced before her eyes until she couldn't doubt it any longer. He had a right to know. But how could she dump that news on him now?

How could she not?

The intercom on her desk buzzed. She pushed the button. "Yes, Connie?"

"Mr. Marchetti is here to see you."

"Send him in," she said, then clicked off.

Moments later her office door opened, and in he walked. She was vaguely surprised that he wasn't wearing business attire since it was the middle of the workday. But she had to admit his worn jeans and the black T-shirt that hugged his broad chest and muscular biceps could redefine *business casual*. As far as the females in the workforce were concerned.

The room seemed to shrink when he stood in front of her desk. Suddenly she didn't have enough oxygen, and it wouldn't have mattered if she had a tank of the stuff hooked up to a mask over her face. Besides it was a flammable chemical and could create a dangerous situation. Whenever she and Luke were in the same room they set off sparks like burning logs shifting in the fireplace. The stage was set for a monumental conflagration—emotional, personal, professional.

"Hello, Luke. How are you?"

"How do you think I am?"

She studied his face, the dark circles under his eyes, the deep creases bracketing his nose and mouth. He looked so tired. In spite of all her self-warnings, her heart went out to him before she could snatch it back. "Are you sleeping? You look awful."

"Thanks very much," he said, one corner of his mouth quirking up. He sat in one of the powder-blue barrel-backed chairs in front of her desk. "That's the pot calling the kettle black. You don't look so hot yourself."

There was a reason for that, but she couldn't just blurt it out. He would start to think she was Typhoid Mary. Every time he saw her she told him something life altering. He would start avoiding her like the plague. That might be for the best, she thought, as at the same time something deep inside her protested.

"I'm fine. Busy." She laced her trembling fingers together and rested her clasped hands on the paperwork piled on her desk. "What can I do for you?"

"I want to discuss the will."

"You talked to your mother?"

He nodded. "She confirmed that Brad Stephenson is my biological father."

"I'm so sorry, Luke. I know it will take some time for you to deal with all the ramifications—"

"Like his estate," he said crisply. "We should get business out of the way first."

She ignored his implication that he had a second reason for being there. Probably personal. She had to nip that in the bud. But disregarding the wave of heat radiating through her at the very idea was considerably more difficult. "I'll buzz Nate McDonald," she said starting to reach for the phone. "I'll send you down the hall to his office if he's available. He has the file."

Luke leaned forward and stopped her with a soft touch from his large, warm hand. "I want you."

A shiver raced over her arm and down her back from the physical contact, but mostly from the intensity in his gaze, focusing so unwaveringly on her. She swallowed hard. "I can't. We already talked about this."

"Okay," he said, nodding with resignation. "I need to grovel. I suppose I deserve it." He gently squeezed her hand, then removed his own. "I apologize for doubting you. I should never have questioned your honesty and integrity."

"Apology unnecessary but gladly accepted," she said, missing the warmth of his touch.

"Thanks. You're very magnanimous. Now about the will. Do you want—"

She shook her head. "You don't understand, Luke. I appreciate the fact that you realize I wasn't lying to you. But that doesn't change anything. It's best for you to see my associate."

"Why?"

"You know why," she said.

"Tell me again." His mouth straightened to a grim line.

"All right." She did her best to rein in her runaway emotions, not an easy feat when pregnancy hormones were thrown into the mix. "There must be absolute trust between attorney and client. If you could entertain the slightest doubt that I was telling you the truth, it's best if you see someone else."

"You have to admit what you told me was a shocker. If Mother Teresa had dropped that bombshell on me I'd have called her a liar."

"But you didn't sleep with her." She looked at her clasped hands as heat suffused her cheeks. It was hard to maintain the upper hand while she sat there with humiliation in living color on her face. "It was a mistake. We can't take it back. And it compromised our association. It changed everything."

Boy did it ever. Tell him now, she thought. It would be relatively simple to segue into "You're not going to believe what happened." But the expression on his face stopped her. It was a look somewhere between anger and pain, laced with a healthy dose of irritation. She'd never seen anyone drowning, but Luke's face showed her what a man would look like going down for the third time. Not now, she decided. She just couldn't bring herself to do it yet.

"Look, Maddie, I just found out everything familiar to me is a fabrication. I don't understand any of it—"

"It will take some time. But there's no doubt in my mind that your parents love you. I think they were just trying to protect you."

"That's what she said."

"Your mother?" she asked, chilled by the coldness in his tone. "You don't believe her?"

"Why should I? She cheated on Tom and passed me off as his son all these years. Give me one good reason why I should believe her now, Maddie."

She didn't have the heart to correct him on the nickname. "Put yourself in her shoes, Luke. Wouldn't you try to do what was best for everyone involved?" Madison folded her arms across her abdomen. She was beginning to understand a mother's protectiveness toward the tiny new life she carried. "She's your mother. Isn't that reason enough to trust her to do what's best for everyone, including an innocent baby?"

"Truth is the most important thing. Up front and as soon as possible."

She winced at his sharp tone. "You think that now. But things aren't always black-and-white. Just wait until you have children of your own."

His eyes went hard and cold. "I don't ever want kids."

Her heart skipped a beat, followed by a crushing pain that stole her breath. "You don't mean that."

"The hell I don't. Why would I want to bring a kid into this world? What could I give him? I don't know who I am, and the people I once trusted aren't who I thought."

"All the more reason for you to see my associate." That would give her time to catch her breath from the blow he'd just dealt her.

He stood up and set his palms on her desk as he leaned close. The fragrance of his aftershave drifted to her mixed with the essence of Luke. She'd spent just a single night in his arms, yet she remembered it so well. But in the flesh Luke was so much more compelling than her memories. If she spent time with him, how was she supposed to resist him? Yet he'd just told her he didn't want children. Why would he want her? No, she had to keep her distance. The potential for pain was too great. Somehow she would pull herself together. Somehow she would tell him because it was the right thing to do. He had the right to know. But that time wasn't now.

"Maddie, listen to me. I'm sorry I didn't believe you. But you caught me off guard. This is the bottom line— you're the one person who had the guts to tell me the truth. I know you always will. I need that now more than ever. I don't want a stranger. I want you."

In spite of the curve he'd just thrown her, she felt his pain. She wanted to ignore her instinctive caution and give him what he needed. She almost blurted out that she would handle the matter. But spending time with him would be a disaster. The attraction hadn't abated. On the contrary, it was stronger. At least on her part. They smoldered together. They could go up in flames without warning. It happened once; it would happen again. She was certain of it.

But she had a new little someone depending on her and her alone. Especially since Luke had made it clear that he didn't want to be a part of the experience. Now, more than ever, it was important for her to build her career. Before it had been about justifying her own existence, showing the world that it could be a better place for her having been here. Now her job was about someone else's well-being. A dalliance with one of the firm's most influential clients was ethical gray area. But it could derail her career plan as easily as saying, "fiduciary responsibility."

A small voice inside her said putting him off was more about protecting her heart. She *was* in charge of the Marchetti business file. But what he was asking her to do was personal, not business. It was her call whether or not to take it on.

"Luke, I can't handle this matter for you. We crossed a line. There's no way to go back, and neither one of us wants to go forward—"

"Speak for yourself."

She stared at him. "That's it. That's the reason right there."

"What reason?"

"Why I can't handle this. You put a personal spin on everything."

"You're in charge of the Marchetti business—" He stopped, and his blue eyes went cold. "Is it because I'm not a Marchetti?"

"Don't be ridiculous. No matter who your father was, you're still the same exasperating man you always were."

He grinned. "I knew you would do this for me. Why don't you get the file and we can go over it. We can order in lunch. I'll buy and—"

It would be so easy to let him sweep her away. Just like that night. But she couldn't afford to lose her grasp on objectivity. She had to keep her eye on the ball. Her career was so much more important than ever before.

"No, Luke. It would be best if you talk to Nate about this. Let me call him in—"

He straightened and backed one step away from her desk. When she had the courage to meet his gaze, winter was back in his eyes.

"Forget it, Maddie."

Without saying anything else, he turned and walked out of her office. She would have felt better if he'd yelled at her and slammed the door. She would have felt better if he'd slid her his boyish grin, his seductive smile, his wolfish, hang-on-to-your-hat-here-I-come expression. All of the above she could handle. But that look of abject desolation made her feel like the worst despicable lawyer joke she'd ever heard.

"Oh, Luke. Please don't do anything desperate."

From the picture windows in his family room, Luke stared down at the lights in the San Fernando Valley north of Los Angeles. A vision of Maddie came to him. There was something so fragile about her. Was that why he couldn't stay angry at her for turning him down?

That feeling didn't extend to his parents. He didn't blame Tom, except for the conspiracy of silence. But his mother... How could she sleep with another man, then live a lie? Worse, how could she let *him* live a lie?

Anger still burned hot in him, but before he could explore it further, the doorbell rang. Maddie had turned her back on him. There wasn't anyone he was expecting or even wanted to see. He was tempted to ignore whoever was there, but something made him curious.

He opened the door and was surprised to see Maddie, holding a large brown bag. Before he could stop it, a sensation of pleasure welled up inside him.

"Hi," he said. He pulled the door wide. "Come on in."

"Thanks."

"You brought food if my sense of smell is still working." He sniffed. "And I'm guessing it didn't come from a Marchetti restaurant."

"I was craving Chinese." Her sweet, hesitant smile burrowed inside him and surrounded his heart.

"Then I'm guessing you're going to join me?" At her

nod, he took the bag from her. "Let's go into the kitchen."

"Okay."

Her heels clicked on the entryway tile as she followed him, then went silent when they got to the plush beige living room carpet.

"I like your furniture," she said, wryly commenting on the empty space. "It allows one's imagination free rein."

"I haven't had a chance to furnish the room yet."

"How long have you lived here?"

"A couple of years."

"Ah. I see your dilemma of time versus motivation." She slid him a saucy look. "Maybe you haven't heard. There's a handy little invention called a decorator. You just pick up the phone, tell them what you want and they do all the footwork. It can be done from the convenience of home or office."

He glanced down at her and couldn't help grinning. "Is that sass? From my attorney?"

"I'm not your attorney," she reminded him.

In the kitchen, he set the bag on the tile of the center island and pulled two plates from the cupboard closest to the nook where the table sat.

"Sell it somewhere else, Counselor. Why else would you be here with food?"

"A peace offering." She pulled several white cartons from the bag and started opening them. "Where do you hide serving utensils?"

"Why? Are you planning to cut my heart out with a spoon?"

"As appealing as that sounds," she said, wrinkling her cute little freckle-dotted nose, "I just thought it would be easier than scooping up dinner with our hands.''

"The only spoons I have are in the drawer below where I keep the plates,'' he said, not moving an inch from in front of that very spot.

"I didn't come here as your attorney.'' Head tipped engagingly to the side, she stared up at him, and her teasing look faded.

There was a wary expression in her eyes, as if she didn't want to move that close to him to get what she was after. But she finally did and stood in front of him waiting for him to move. He took a deep breath, drawing in the sweet, flowery, innocent scent of her. It went straight inside him and made his blood flow hot through his veins.

Reluctantly he stepped to the side so she could reach in the drawer. "Why did you come, Maddie?''

She stuck spoons in the beef and broccoli and the fried rice, then met his gaze. "I wanted to make sure you were okay.''

"Why wouldn't I be?''

She snorted. "Don't go macho on me, Luke. I saw the look in your eyes when you walked out of my office earlier.''

"What look?''

"The last time I checked, you were smarter than the average bear. I think you know what I'm talking about. I'd rather have macho than moron.''

"Moron?'' he said, his mouth twitching as he tried not to laugh.

He liked the way she met him—tough instead of touchy-feely. A straight talker, his Maddie. No, not his. She'd made that clear. And did he even want her to be his?

He'd never been in love. He'd reached a point where he considered the merits of just settling for someone as opposed to being alone. Then everything went crazy. Maddie had given him her innocence and what was probably the best night of his life. Then he'd found out his father wasn't his father. Right now he didn't know what he wanted, especially in the relationship department. All he could think about was this moment. And at this moment he was awfully damn glad Maddie Wainright was here.

"Don't play dumb. It's pretty unattractive. You walked out of my office like a thunderstorm ready to drop baseball-size hail on Encino."

"You were worried about me," he guessed. Inside he was doing a high-five.

"Good heavens, no."

"You're not a good liar, Maddie."

"No? I thought the world-at-large perceived lawyers to be the best liars."

He wondered why her expression changed from saucy to studiously blank. He wondered why he even noticed or how he knew her well enough to identify the look.

"This isn't about your profession. Admit it. You were afraid I would do something rash, reckless."

"Puhleeze," she said, rolling her eyes. "Don't be so dramatic. I merely stopped by with food because you have to eat."

He'd filled a plate, then set it on the table and stood beside it while he waited for her. "Okay, Counselor," he said, crossing his arms over his chest. "Your job is to wrestle the truth from witnesses. Mine is numbers. And my guess is there's a 99.9 percent chance that you're here because you have a guilty conscience."

She dropped the spoon as her gaze snapped to his so

fast he thought she would get whiplash. And her face went chalk white. "Wh-why would I feel guilty?"

"Because you turned down my request to handle Brad Stephenson's estate."

She finished putting a paltry amount of food on her plate, then joined him at the table. He came around and held her chair as she sat at a right angle to him. "I suppose that's true. And I wanted to make sure you were all right. You looked so—desperate—I wasn't sure what you might do."

"I'm really okay," he said.

"I see that. But don't guys drive too fast when they're upset? Do self-destructive things? I wanted to be certain you made it home."

"Um, Maddie, there's this handy little invention called the telephone." He mimicked her earlier teasing tone. "You pick it up, dial my number, and if I answer, I'm okay."

"I needed to see you," she blurted out.

The words, unrehearsed, straight from her heart warmed him clear to his battered soul. "And do I look all right?" he asked, meeting her gaze.

Her green eyes widened slightly, and her breathing quickened just a fraction. In a voice that was just a bit unsteady, she said, "You look fine," she said, almost whispering the last word.

"Is there another reason you needed to see me?" he guessed.

She put her fork down after moving the food around her plate. "Yes. I want to make certain you understand and are okay with why I can't handle this legal matter for you."

He was about to say he understood. She'd explained that it was business and the night they'd spent together precluded them from their former working relationship. He didn't like it one single bit, but he got it. Then he noticed a little-girl-lost look in her eyes. Something told him to let her talk.

He put his fork down. "Okay. I'm listening."

"It's about my parents."

He put his hand over his heart and three fingers up in the Boy Scout salute. "I swear I never did anything to them if that's why you're cutting me loose."

She laughed. "I'm not accusing you of anything. Talk about a guilty conscience. And why does it always have to be about you? Has anyone ever told you that you're self-absorbed?"

"Hey, I'm having a personal crisis, slick." It felt so good to tease. Maddie was the only one he felt he could be like that with. He needed that now. She was good for him. "If you came here to stroke my ego and make me feel better, you're not doing a very good job."

"I need to tell you about me so you'll understand why I have to take myself off your file." She took a deep breath. "You know I have a brother. He's six years older. He was the obligatory heir my mother was *required* to produce. He was in school and she was happily pursuing her own thing when she found out she was pregnant."

"With you."

"I once overheard her tell my father that I was an accident." She drew in a deep breath. "By definition that's an unforeseen, unwanted event resulting from carelessness. A nonessential property."

How could anyone not want her? Nonessential? She was pretty important to him. That message had come through loud and clear when she'd refused to handle his legal affairs. But this was about her.

"It happens. That doesn't mean they don't love you," he protested.

She had such an odd, half-hopeful, half-forlorn expression on her face. Damn, he wanted to pull her into his arms and tell her it was true. Not only that, *he* wanted her. But he knew it wasn't what she needed just then. With a supreme effort of will, he sat without moving. "Of course they love you."

She shrugged. "In their own way. Maybe. But that meant nannies and boarding school. Now they're on the east coast and I'm on the west. And never the twain shall meet. The point is, my career is very important to me."

He couldn't help feeling she'd stopped short of saying it was all she had. "You don't need to justify your existence."

"Yes, I—" She stopped, then clasped her hands so tightly her knuckles turned white. "How did you know that?"

"I minored in psych in college. I needed to balance the math classes." His father—Tom, he mentally corrected—had suggested that. "You're a vital, valuable woman. Period."

She twisted her fingers together. "Intellectually I know you're right. But in my heart, I need to do something worthwhile. Maybe pro bono work, legal aid. Help people who can't afford counsel. I'm on the fast track at the firm. The higher I go, the more I can do."

"What does that have to do with representing me?"

"We can't go back to the way things were before—" she stopped and briefly met his gaze "—that night. And we can't go forward with a personal association. Neither of us wants that. You're a confirmed bachelor."

"Is that so?" Why did her assessment yank his chain?

"Of course. If you had wanted to settle down, you'd

have done it by now. And I'm committed to my career and the power that success can give me. That cancels out moving forward.''

''I still don't see what that has to do with handling the details of my late father's estate.''

''You refuse to see. If I take care of your file, we would be working together. A lot. I can't take the chance that our business dealings could take a personal turn and jeopardize my job. I told you once before that at the very least it's the suggestion of impropriety.''

''You make a good case. And you're right. I choose not to see. Because you're a talented and gifted attorney. Two reasons why I need you to help me.''

''What's the third?''

He waited to answer, long enough to let her gaze swing to his and lock there. ''Good or bad, you know who your parents are. I never had the opportunity to meet my biological father, let alone get to know him. Now I never will. I won't have the chance to like or dislike him. To try to be different—or the same.''

''To win his love?'' she asked gently.

His gaze shot to hers, and he was relieved there was no pity in it. Nothing but gentleness. Sweetness. He could wrap himself in her softness if only she would let him. But he knew her reference to love was about herself and her ongoing battle with parents who didn't show it. Or as she believed, just didn't feel it. He wanted to throttle them. She would be so easy to love. He'd been drawn to her two years ago, the first time they met. Something about her still pulled him now. But emotionally, he had nothing to give her.

''This isn't about love, Maddie. It's about finding out who I am. I've lost my family. I don't have any of the people I used to have. My support system is gone. I don't even have the opportunity to confront the guy who is half responsible for the hell I'm living. You are the only constant in my life.''

"Luke, that's not true. You have—"

"It feels true. It's as true as you believing you have to validate your existence. You're the only one I have left. I'm asking you to help me with this.''

She stood and walked to the sliding glass doors, staring at the lights of the valley for a long time. Her shoulders slumped, and finally she turned. ''I have one condition.''

"Anything."

"It has to be strictly business. I mean it, Luke. Nothing personal. At all. We can't do wh-what we did. Never again. Lawyer, client. End of story.''

"Okay."

"I mean it. I want your word."

"If I had a Bible, I would swear on it."

"I can't do this," she said, shaking her head. "You're making a joke out of it." She started for the front door.

He intercepted her easily and stopped her with his hands on her shoulders. Gently he tightened his grip until she lifted her gaze to his.

"Maddie, if I don't joke I'm going to crack into a million pieces. Humor is keeping me sane. And you're the one person I can count on for what I need—humor, teasing, and most important of all—the truth. Cut me some slack, okay? I don't want anything personal any more than you do. My life is a shambles. Do you think I have room for a relationship? You have my word that there will be nothing between us but business.''

"Okay." She nodded. "And you have my word that I'll handle this matter to the best of my ability. With integrity, discretion and honesty.''

Chapter Four

"Let's finish dinner," Luke suggested, "Now that everything is settled."

Not by a long shot, Madison thought.

He'd just said he didn't have room for a personal relationship. He'd also said his life was a shambles and he didn't want kids. Now was not the time to tell him he was going to be a father. She couldn't do it. Not yet.

Just agreeing to handle his father's will was a major step. Was it emotional suicide? How often would she have to see him? How many meetings would it take to discharge all the details of his father's estate? Could she muster enough willpower to keep from throwing herself into his arms? At what point did she tell him that she was going to have his baby?

She studied him. He looked more relaxed than when she'd first arrived. Amused and more lighthearted which made her very happy. Imagine that.

The creases bracketing his nose and mouth had resumed their function as dimples. He'd focused his intensity on her, and what she saw in his expression made her knees as weak as an unsuccessful batch of meringue.

He was almost smiling. And why not? He'd gotten his way. His blue eyes sparkled with humor again. God help her, she couldn't bring herself to pull the rug out from under him with the news about the baby. Not just yet. After the will reading was behind them she would tell him for sure.

With his knuckle, he gently raised her chin. "Where are you? Earth to Maddie?"

She'd asked him to call her Madison and she couldn't remember a single time that he had. Luke was a rule breaker. That didn't bode well for his promise to keep their relationship strictly business.

"Yo, Counselor."

She shook her head to clear it. "Sorry. What did you say?"

"Let's finish dinner. After all, you were the one craving Chinese food."

Her cheeks grew warm. What in the world had made her use that exact word—*craving?* Even though it had been the truth. "Okay."

"You hardly ate anything. Is something wrong?"

"No." Technically that was true. In spite of the circumstances, and contrary to normal rational thought processes, she was happy about the baby. She had an appointment with an obstetrician. But according to the books she'd read, feeling as if she had a chronic case of the flu was normal. Suddenly the thought of food was about as appealing as having all four wisdom teeth pulled. And how did she keep that to herself with the full force of his head-turning masculine attention focused on her?

Luke frowned at her. "Are you sure you're all right?

In spite of the fact that I'm self-absorbed, I have noticed that you look a little pale lately. Or, to quote a recent statement from someone I respect very much, you look awful.''

"Thank you," she said. So much for pregnancy making her beautiful and suffusing her with that special glow. "It's just female stuff. Trust me, you don't want to know."

That was all true. He wouldn't want to know, because he didn't want kids.

They walked back into the kitchen and he held her chair while she sat. "You're quite the gentleman."

He sat down beside her and his eyes darkened. "My father—I mean Tom—drilled it into Nick, Joe, Alex and me. My brothers—half brothers," he amended.

"Which half?"

"What?" He slid her an odd look.

"Which half is still your brother?" she picked up a fortune cookie. "The head? Hands? Feet? Shoulders? Hair?"

"That's ridiculous."

"Exactly. They're not your brothers in fractions. I know them. They don't do things by halves. It's all or nothing. You, too, by the way."

He ignored that and went on. "We learned to always open the door for a lady, hold her chair, carry packages. Why didn't I ever notice that I was different?"

"In what way?"

"Besides the eyes, there were personality differences."

"Such as?"

"Off the top of my head, the whole confirmed-bachelor thing."

"What are you talking about?"

"We always joked about it. But the truth is, unlike me, Nick, Joe and Alex were looking. They had relationships before finding their respective wives. Nick with the waitress when the business branched out into Phoenix and he opened the first restaurant there. He secretly married her when he found out she was pregnant by another man. Then she went back to her baby's father and had it annulled."

She nodded. "I heard about that. And Alex lost his college sweetheart, then figured he'd had his one and only chance at love."

"And he wouldn't get another."

"Until Fran," she reminded him.

"Right. And I found out Joe was looking but afraid to take a chance on love because as a little kid he remembered seeing Mom cry. When she and Tom were having problems. Which is when I came into the picture," he added. "But Joe watched his friends' marriages fall apart, and that kept him from committing to a woman."

"Until Liz," she commented.

"True. But unlike my brothers who walked the walk, the talk they talked was macho doublespeak. I think I really am a confirmed bachelor. I've never met a woman who made me want to take the next step." He met her gaze, and the intense look in his eyes made her hot all over.

Was he trying to tell her something? That she shouldn't expect a commitment from him?

"I'm different from them, Maddie. Maybe I'm not capable of committing to a woman. Obviously the Marchetti men are. Not to mention my sister, Rosie, who fell in love with Steve Schafer when they were practically kids. But I'm not like them because I'm not one of them.''

''Does the phrase *product of your environment* mean anything to you?''

''Of course.''

''You were raised the same as your brothers and sister. Your father pounded the gentlemanly arts into you along with love, commitment and family values. No matter what problems occurred in your parents' marriage, they got past them and have been a devoted couple ever since. Your brothers picked up on that and when they found the right woman it was magic. It will happen with you, too.''

Although she couldn't say the same for herself. Even if she could fall in love, the road for her and Luke had too many speed bumps to overcome. A detour around each other was the smart way to go.

He didn't look at all convinced. ''I don't think so. It could be a chemistry thing. Something I inherited from my father, an inability to fall in love and commit.''

''I still put my money on environment.''

She should know. She was a product of cold surroundings where showing emotion just wasn't done. And that was before boarding school, where people were paid to care for her because it was their job. Madison knew love wasn't in her past or future because she didn't know how. Although she was beginning to feel a stirring of it for her baby and suspected the sensation would only get stronger. But that was entirely different from the man-woman kind of feelings.

''Tom and Flo love each other,'' she said. ''And they love their kids. You can't grow up with that and not learn how to do it.''

''I did.''

"You're choosing to ignore the feelings."

"Can we change the subject?" he asked, rubbing a hand across the back of his neck.

"Okay."

That suited her just fine. Love was the last thing she wanted to discuss. Especially with the only man who had ever swept her away. The only one who had successfully made her lose control. She suspected he could do it again with very little trouble. How? Why? What made him different from the other guys who had tried?

"What do you want to talk about?" He scooped up a forkful of beef and broccoli.

"How's work? What's going on at Marchetti's Incorporated?" she asked, grabbing the most innocuous subject she could think of. But when a shadow crossed his face, she knew she'd struck a nerve somehow.

"I haven't been to the office since finding out the truth."

"Luke! You're joking."

He shook his head. "I'm not sure I'll ever go back."

A good lawyer learned when to speak and when to listen. A good lawyer maintained objectivity in order to advise a client. In her heart she believed it would be a mistake for him to turn his back on the business. At the same time, if he did, she would need to counsel him in negotiating a severance, stock options earned during his years with the company and other benefits that he had accrued.

Madison worked hard at being a good attorney and took her responsibility to her clients very seriously. But at the moment she wished for the world's biggest roll of duct tape to keep from asking if he was crazy.

Instead she asked, "Why?" Then she bit the corner

of her lip to keep any more words from coming out of her mouth.

"I can't believe you're even asking me that. Isn't it obvious?"

"Not to me. You're CFO of the company. Based on the success of the business, I'm guessing you do a pretty fair job."

"Careful. Flattery like that will turn my head."

"Your head is too big to turn anymore," she said with a fleeting grin. "Your family expects you to show up for work. Why would anything change for them?"

"Because I'm not Tom Marchetti's son."

"So after thirty years they're going to stop loving you because your DNA isn't what they thought? And you can stop loving them?"

"This is a big deal, Maddie. Why do you refuse to see it?" There was a desperation in his voice that tore at her heart.

She had to touch him. Bracing herself for the inevitable heat, she put her hand on his forearm. But she wasn't prepared for him to remove her hand, then place it in his palm and intertwine their fingers. The warmth swept up her arm and settled in her chest, making her breasts swell. Her brain seemed to overheat and shut down. She couldn't seem to get enough air into her lungs.

She took a deep breath to counteract oxygen deprivation. "I...I know it's a big deal. I'm not trying to minimize the magnitude of this. But sometimes it takes someone sort of removed to be objective. In the prim, proper, appearance-is-the-only-thing Wainright family, this would be a big deal. But not yours. Nothing is going to change the fact that they love you."

"They love who they thought I was."

"You're not Jekyll and Hyde. You're still the same man you were before you found out. You're still the same son and brother that they love." She put her other hand over their joined fingers. "God help me for crossing this line but I'm going to say it, anyway. You would be crazy to turn your back on the people who love you and leave such a successful business."

"*Family* business." He pulled his hand from hers and ran his fingers through his hair. "And I'm not part of the family. I know you're not into fractions, but being half a family member isn't good enough."

She picked up a piece of her fortune cookie and put it in her mouth. Slowly she chewed, hoping it would act like the crackers that the books said would settle her stomach.

"Luke, I've probably already said too much—"

He shook his head. "I count on you to tell me the truth even when I don't want to hear it. Why do you think I fought so hard to convince you to be my attorney?"

Would he change his mind if he knew she was carrying his baby and hadn't told him right away?

"What were you going to say?" he asked, placing her hand between his own.

"Why are you so sure they're going to write you off? If any of the others was going through this, would you turn your back?"

"No, but I'm not turning my back on them, just pulling myself out of the business."

She realized he was backing off for himself, to deal with it. If *he* let the family go, it might not hurt so much in the event they did reject him.

She could play his game. "I think you're going to

have an uphill battle convincing the Marchettis that you're not a member of the family.''

"You're wrong, Maddie. They'll be relieved if I just disappear.''

"Want to bet?''

One corner of his mouth turned up, chasing away his dark expression. ''Sure. If I can name the stakes.''

His eyes took on a challenging, sexy expression. She knew that look. She'd seen it once before, the moment before he'd kissed her senseless and had taken her with him on an unforgettable journey of passion. She couldn't take that trip with him again.

"Don't go there, Luke. Remember I said this is strictly business.'' She tried to pull her hand away.

He held it gently but firmly. ''You started it. Besides, who says the stakes have to be personal? Twenty bucks says the Marchettis will breathe a sigh of relief when I walk away.''

"You're on,'' she said. ''When do you want to schedule a reading of the will?'' Her stomach clenched. She knew once that was over she would have to tell him her news.

"Day after tomorrow?''

So soon? she thought. But she nodded. ''That will give me a day to familiarize myself with the file.''

"Put me on your calendar. I'll look forward to seeing you then, Maddie.''

She let out a long breath. If only it would be long enough to help her find the right words to tell him what she needed to.

"Luke Marchetti is here to see you.''

Madison pressed the intercom button. ''Send him in.''

Several moments later her office door opened. In

strode Luke. His casual attire instantly told her he hadn't changed his mind about going back to work. The jeans molded to his lean hips and muscular thighs in a supremely masculine way. She remembered him saying that she could sway judge, jury and opposing counsel if she wore jeans to court. The delicious memory, along with the even more delicious man in front of her made her heart beat like the wings of a frightened bird. He could have her in the palm of his hand with a flash of his dimples and she would do everything in her power to keep him from knowing that.

"Hi, Luke." She held out her hand to indicate the chairs in front of her desk. "Have a seat."

"Thanks."

She sat down, too, and took a deep breath. "I tried to get in touch with you. Have you stopped picking up your messages?"

"Lately, yeah." He folded his arms over his chest. "What did you need to tell me?"

"I wanted to warn you that your mother will be present at this meeting."

"What? Why?" He asked standing. His expression went from easygoing to I'm-outta-here in zero point three seconds.

"I guess that'll teach you to check your voice mail. Flo will be here momentarily, per your father's instructions. He left something for her in the file."

"I don't want to see her."

"Then I can't proceed. It's my responsibility to carry out his last wishes." She folded her hands. "As your lawyer, and friend, let me advise you to get it over with. You've put your whole life on hold. You can't move forward until you get this behind you. And you can't do that until the will is read."

The intercom buzzed. "Yes?" Madison answered, after pushing the button.

"Mrs. Marchetti is here."

Madison looked at Luke. He nodded curtly. "Send her in," she said.

A moment later Flo walked into the office. She looked tired, older. There were lines on her face Madison had never seen before.

"Hello, Madison. Luke," she said. She studied him with what Madison somehow knew was a mother's all-seeing eyes. "You look tired, Son. Are you taking care of yourself?"

"I'm fine," he answered. His voice was carefully devoid of emotion, as was his face.

Watching the two of them tugged at Madison's heart. She'd seen them together and had always envied the close relationship. She'd never had anything even remotely resembling it with her mother. And *remote* was definitely the operative word. Her father? Forget it. Would it be better to know what it was like and lose it or to never know what it felt like at all?

"Won't you both sit down, please?" Madison asked.

When they did, she opened the file, then looked from Flo to Luke. They could look stiffer, but she wasn't sure how. She'd been in awkward situations before, but never had the words *cut the tension with a knife* been more true.

She cleared her throat. "Mr. Stephenson left each of you a letter," she began.

From the file she took two sealed envelopes and handed the appropriate one to Luke, then his mother.

Flo's hand shook when she took hers. "Am I to read it now?"

"That's up to you," Madison explained. But she noticed that Luke put his in his shirt pocket.

Luke's mother glanced at the handwritten note, then looked up. "If it's all right with you, Madison and Luke," she said, glancing at him, "I'd like to read it aloud."

When Madison nodded and Luke shrugged, the woman began:

"Dear Florence, if you're reading this, it means I'm gone. When the doctors diagnosed the cancer, I knew it was just a matter of time. I know we agreed that it was best for our son and your children that you and Tom raise him as your own. Forgive me, Flo, but as my time on earth grows short, I just can't bear the thought that I will cease to exist without him knowing about me—"

Flo's voice cracked, and she stopped to compose herself.

Madison studied Luke's expression for a sign of his feelings. He still wore the same dark, angry look.

After several moments she continued.

"I had to leave everything I'd acquired in my life to my only child, my son. Luke. That means he has to know about me—us. I am so very sorry. I hope someday you and Tom can find it in your hearts to forgive me. Always, Brad."

Flo looked up. "That explains why he changed our agreement when we all decided it would be best—"

"How did you figure that would be best for me?"

Luke said, his voice humming with anger. "All that solution did was protect you from disgrace."

"I couldn't care less how scandal would touch me. But, yes, I was concerned about how it would affect my children and the new baby I carried."

"Right," he said sarcastically.

Madison wanted to jump in and help Flo make her case. But this was one of those times to keep quiet.

Flo folded the letter and put it in her purse. "Think about it, Luke. It would have been worse than a divorce situation with joint custody." She half turned toward him. "Visitations with your biological father would have set you apart within the family unit. Children need to feel wanted and loved and as if they have a place to fit."

Madison could relate to that. "It makes sense, Luke."

He flashed her an angry glare, then met his mother's gaze. "So I grew up thinking I was a Marchetti. How does that make it all right?"

"Brad agreed that it was best for you and promised to stay out of your life. Although, after reading his letter, I see now how unfair it was to him."

"And to Tom," Luke ground out.

"Yes," she said, nodding miserably. "And most of all to you. But I was a young mother with three little boys. I hardly ever saw your—Tom. Every waking moment was spent working to expand the business." She reached out a hand to touch him, but when he shot her a look, she let it fall without making contact. "Your father, Brad, was handsome, charming and attentive. He made me feel attractive and cherished at a time when I desperately needed it."

"And that excuses your behavior?" he asked.

"Nothing could do that. I just want to try to make

you understand. The mistake was mine and mine alone. Tom loves you. Don't blame him for—''

''The only thing I blame him for is letting me believe I was someone I'm not.''

Flo sat up straight, and her eyes flashed with emotion. ''You are his son. He walked the floor with you when you were a teething infant. He attended every single solitary sporting event you ever played, from high school football to T-ball, even though you stood in the outfield, plopped your mitt on your head and picked grass. He was at the hospital when you were eighteen and had your broken ankle pinned. He held you when the pain was so bad you cried, while you waited for the medication to kick in. He was your father when it wasn't easy or fun. But he welcomed all of it because he loves you.'' She stopped to take a deep breath. ''Don't you dare criticize his actions. His motives are unimpeachable.''

Luke rubbed a hand over his face. ''I will never understand how he could know what you did and not walk out.''

Flo's mouth thinned, then she stood. ''Then you're an idiot. In spite of that, you're a Marchetti, my son, and a member of the family.''

Without another word, she walked to the door, opened it, and left the room.

Madison looked at Luke. ''Well, that could have gone worse. Although I'm not sure how.''

''If I had known she would be here—''

''If you hadn't turned into a world-class hermit—''

''So this is my fault?'' he asked.

''You could be more conciliatory.''

''Don't sit in judgment of me, Maddie. How would you feel if you were in my shoes?''

''You mean if I found out I was adopted and there

was someone out there who cared enough about me to put my needs above everything else? I'd do the dance of joy.''

His eyes narrowed. ''You have no idea what I'm going through.''

''Being loved more than life itself?'' She nodded. ''That's true. I don't. But your mother is only human. Everyone makes mistakes. Even you.''

''Yes, but I—''

The intercom buzzed. ''I'm still in a meeting,'' Madison told her secretary.

''Sorry. Mrs. Marchetti left, and I just assumed you were finished. There's a phone call.''

''What is it?'' Madison asked. Since they'd already been interrupted, she might as well see what was so important.

''The doctor's office is on the line. They want to confirm your appointment.''

Madison's heart jumped into her throat. She went hot all over as she looked at Luke and noted the intensity of his gaze. ''Tell them I'll return the call later, Connie.''

''Is something wrong?'' Luke asked. Concern made his eyes dark.

She couldn't help the glad little ripple that went through her. Had anyone ever been concerned about her that way? If so, she couldn't remember who or when. ''No.''

''You didn't eat enough to keep a bird alive when we had dinner the other night. And that day in my office you were dizzy.''

''I'm fine. It's a checkup,'' she explained. Now, she thought. Tell him. She had the perfect opening.

He stood up. ''Okay. If you're sure. I have to go.''

''But I haven't read the will yet.''

"Right now I don't care if it ever gets read."

"You don't mean that."

"You're wrong. I've never meant anything more." He walked to the door and stopped with his hand on the knob. Then he glanced at her over his shoulder. "As far as I'm concerned, Maddie, nothing she said makes a difference. That twenty bucks is still mine."

Chapter Five

While he waited for Maddie, Luke glanced at his kitchen table one last time. Flowers—check. Wine—check. Candles—check. No flame yet, but it wouldn't be long. She would be here any minute. She could pretend that there was nothing personal between them. But if that were true, she wouldn't have arranged to come to his house tonight. And he was glad she had. When they were together, electricity crackled and things heated up. Especially him.

The doorbell rang. "Here's Miss Hot-and-Bothered now."

He went to the door. It had been a week since that disastrous meeting in her office. Seven days of thinking about what his mother had said without being able to understand. Seven days and nights of no contact with Maddie. Suddenly he needed to see her like a parched man needs water.

He opened the door. "Hi. Come on in."

"Thanks," she said.

He drank in the sight of her. She wore a floral print cotton jumper with a soft white T-shirt underneath. And sandals. Her toenails were painted orangey-red. A scrunchy held her red hair on top of her head, letting the curls cascade to one side, over her ear. Could she possibly be more feminine, he thought. His heart rate cranked up several notches, heating his blood and sending it south, to pool in his groin.

Then he noticed her briefcase and remembered why she was here.

"You brought the will." It wasn't a question.

She nodded. "What changed your mind? Have you read the letter your father left you?"

He shook his head. "But it's time for the will. No guts, no glory. I just called to reschedule the appointment. Who knew my legal eagle was so accommodating? I've been trying to figure out why you insisted on coming to my place."

"Because I need to get this over with, and you can't walk out. It's your house."

"Get this over with?" he questioned.

She had more rules than the IRS, including nothing personal. He figured nothing, including an act of God, could force her to set foot in his house. Had she insisted on dropping by because she was worried about him again? Afraid his state of mind would cause him to drive too fast? He liked that she was concerned about him. From puberty on, the opposite sex had come on to him. He'd been told he wasn't hard to look at, and the fact that he had money drew women. Besides his mother, he couldn't remember a single one who'd cared enough to worry about him.

But he wondered how long it would last. The attraction always faded. It would with Maddie, too. Only a matter of time.

She looked down for a moment, then met his gaze. "'Get this over with' wasn't the best way to put it. But you know what I mean."

"No, I don't. But I'm very interested in this new legal maneuver of yours to get the job done. The do-as-I-say-not-as-I-do method."

"What are you talking about?"

"Me walking out of my house. The strategy won't hold water, Counselor. You were going to walk out on me—when we were at your place. Remember?"

"That was different," she said. Her cheeks turned pink.

When was the last time he'd seen a woman blush? Probably the last time Maddie had heard one of his double entendres. She looked so cute it made him want to tease her some more, to see if he could turn her lovely, smooth skin that same rosy shade.

"Let's go into the kitchen."

She made him hot all over and he needed to take his focus off her. If you can't stand the heat, go *into* the kitchen? The rest of his life was topsy-turvy, why not this?

He reached over to take her briefcase, and their fingers brushed. If it had been pitch-black, he was sure he would have seen a burst of sparks between them. If they were close enough to the candles, they would spontaneously light without the matches he'd set out.

She quickly pulled her hand back. "Thank you."

Her sexy, breathless voice reached inside him and grabbed his primal need in a steely grip that belied her fragile look. He wanted her. Once wasn't enough. He had implied to her that he wanted to go forward with what they'd started. He hadn't changed his mind. But she'd wrung a promise out of him not to pursue anything personal. At least this house call hadn't been his idea. And he was beginning to think it was a bad idea.

It would take precious little to make him break that promise. He was trying like hell to find his emotional equilibrium, and every time he saw her, she turned him inside out and upside down. All it took was a smile, a blush, painted toenails, curls on top of her head and a voice so soft and seductive he could lose his self-control in a heartbeat. If he didn't get a grip, he would be walking out of his house—for Maddie's sake.

He set her briefcase beside the kitchen island. "I've got a lasagne in the oven."

"You didn't need to bother," she said. "This won't take that long."

"No bother. It's one of the new frozen entrées that Alex and Fran developed." Pain shot through him, reminding him he wasn't a part of Marchetti's anymore. Time to change the subject. "It's the least I could do, since you made a house call. And I won't be responsible for you missing a meal. Not on my watch."

"I didn't realize I was anyone's 'watch,'" she said. But the grin on her face told him she wasn't annoyed. In fact, she appeared pleased.

"It's just an expression. But I haven't seen you eat much lately, at least not when you were with me. I'll pour you some wine—"

"No!" Her tone was sharp. His gaze shot to hers and she looked uncomfortable, as if she hadn't meant to speak so abruptly. "I—I mean I want to stay clear-headed. This is business. Remember?"

"If I forgot for a second, there's no doubt in my mind that you would remind me," he said wryly.

But he would like to forget it and for more than a second. He'd like to take her into his bedroom and pick up where they'd left off in hers. What was it about Maddie? She certainly wasn't the most beautiful woman he'd ever known. And she was small and delicate, the complete opposite of his usual willowy, voluptuous type. She wouldn't make the cover of a magazine as the sexiest woman alive. But he couldn't get her out of his mind.

Maybe it was the vulnerability she tried to hide. Or the fact that she wasn't the typical barracuda lawyer type. She wanted to use her knowledge and power to help others. Did she see him as just another charity case?

He took a deep breath. Talk about needing a clear head. Maddie had a way of clouding his thoughts, distracting him, every time they were together. He studied her more closely. She said she was okay, but she wasn't a good liar. He couldn't shake the feeling that something was up with her.

There were circles under her eyes, and her face looked thin. Other than when she blushed, her cheeks were pale. And her vehement refusal of a glass of wine seemed over the top. And what was her rush to get the will reading behind her?

Then his stomach knotted. It was so simple. She wanted to get it over with so she wouldn't have to see him anymore. And the part of him that was thinking with his head realized that would be for the best. She was good for him. Now. She was his anchor in a changing world. But as soon as the crisis was over, the need would disappear. And so would she. That was the way it always worked for him. There was just one problem. The idea of not seeing Maddie made him want to put his fist through the wall.

"I'll serve dinner," he said abruptly.

"Can I help?"

He shook his head. "Just have a seat."

"Okay."

She looked at the elaborate table. "Do you have candles and flowers for all your guests?"

"Only the special ones."

"This isn't a date, Luke."

"If you say so."

Madison sat in the chair with her back to the open sliding glass door. She was only too happy to move away from Luke. When she was close to him, any semblance of deductive reasoning went right out the window. He was constantly on her mind. And when they were in the same room, she felt a physical ache to be in his arms. Maybe if she had never known the magic of letting him possess her. And she'd thought losing her virginity would simplify her life. Ha! If things could get more complicated, she wasn't sure how. And she still wasn't certain why she'd let him be the first. She watched him fill two plates with lasagne, salad and garlic bread. Beneath his black T-shirt, the muscles in his back rippled as he moved. The sleeves of his shirt pulled snugly around his biceps. His jeans sat low on his hips and clung to muscular thighs, making him look all male and trouble with a capital T.

Something fluttered in her chest, and suddenly she found it difficult to breathe. The ache, the physical pain to have him hold her, grew more intense. She had never felt anything like this in her life. She was afraid that he could crush her as easily as a dry leaf.

She had to distract herself. Clearing her throat, she asked, "Have you decided whether or not you're going back to work at Marchetti's?"

With a plate in each hand, he walked to the table and set one in front of her. "Yes."

"Thank you," she said, her eyes growing wide at the amount of food he'd given her. When he sat at a right angle to her, she met his gaze. "Do you want to share the information with me?"

"Not really."

"Okay."

She started to eat, surprised at how hungry she suddenly was. Lusting after a man could sure work up an appetite, she thought. If luck was with her, the lasagne would hit her stomach and not come back up. She wasn't quite ready to have *that* conversation with him. They both ate in silence for a few moments.

Finally he looked at her. "You're not going to push for an answer?"

"About going back to work?" she clarified.

"Yeah," he said, almost angrily.

"You said you didn't want to talk about it."

"Since when have you ever listened to what I wanted?"

She chewed for several moments, then said, "I always listen. I just don't always concur. But I agreed to represent you, didn't I?"

"Yes. After I practically signed the promise in blood."

"Has anyone ever told you that you have a finely developed flair for the dramatic?"

"Yes. And I can't help wondering where I got it," he said tightly. "Since you asked, three days ago I mailed a letter of resignation to Nick."

She put her fork down, stunned at what he'd said. "Oh, Luke. I thought you were going to wait a while before making such an important decision."

He shrugged. "I didn't want to keep them hanging. Now they can hire someone to take my place."

"Are you kidding? They can never replace you."

And she had a bad feeling neither could she. Now that he'd awakened her sexual feelings, could any other man make her feel breathless, hot and cold at the same time, and weak as a newborn colt with a mere flash of his to-die-for dimples? She hoped not. Once her business with Luke was over, she wanted to go back to her well-ordered, both-feet-on-the-ground, one-day-at-a-time world. No more magic for her. Contrary to the fairy tales she'd loved as a little girl, it didn't solve problems. It created them.

Luke chewed his last bite of lasagne thoughtfully, then set his fork on his empty plate. "They would be crazy not to promote my assistant. He's been holding down the fort since I took this leave of absence. They don't need me."

"You're wrong about that. But as I said before, it's difficult to move forward when you're dealing with the past. If you're ready, I'll tell you what's in the will."

He looked at her half-empty plate. "Are you finished eating?" he asked skeptically.

"Yes. And before you start, what you gave me would feed a family of four. It was delicious. And I'm full. So don't get on my case. Your obligation is fulfilled."

"I've got dessert," he said.

Madison's breath caught at the look on his face. Wolf-ish and ingenuous at the same time. He probably had something in the refrigerator with enough calories to sustain a starving, third-world country for a week. But he wanted her to think he meant a treat of a sensual nature. Truthfully, she would give up chocolate for the rest of her life for just a moment in his arms. And that scared her to death.

"About the will," she said standing. "Where did you put my briefcase?"

"By the island." He stood, too, and picked up their plates.

She retrieved her papers and took them to the table. At the same time he cleared off the remains of their dinner and pushed aside flowers and candles.

Madison waited for him to sit, then opened the file and spread out the will in front of her. She glanced through the legal-size pages to be sure she didn't miss any of the high points.

"Here goes." She cleared her throat. "Your father franchised tax and accounting offices."

"He was a businessman?"

She nodded. "An accountant."

"I guess that explains where my propensity for numbers comes from," he said grimly.

Madison refused to get sucked in by emotion. Just give him the details she told herself. Let him assimilate this information. Then she would tell him about the baby. She'd seen the doctor. The pregnancy was confirmed, and Luke had a right to know. For that emotional confrontation she would need all her strength. But one trauma at a time.

She cleared her throat. "He had a sizable estate including property, bank accounts and stock options. There is a cabin in Mammoth Lakes and one in Big Bear, not to mention a small condo near Santa Barbara. He has a membership in an exclusive country club. He never married, and you are his only offspring. It's all yours, Luke. He left everything to you."

"That was pretty straightforward. How come you

didn't just tell me over the phone? Why the formal reading?"

"I wanted to be here—to make sure you were listening," she added, so he wouldn't think it was personal. Even though she couldn't help that it was. "I want this to sink in. Later, you'll have a lot of decisions to make about the business."

"I'm still stuck on the fact that he was into numbers."

She supposed it was natural to wonder where the color of your hair came from. Why you were short or tall. Where did you get a love of reading or athletic ability. Luke had never questioned any of that. He'd never had reason to. Until now.

He stood up so fast his chair nearly toppled over. Without a word he walked to the sliding screen, opened it and walked outside onto the patio. Madison stood, too, and watched him. There was tension in his shoulders. Angrily he ran his hand through his hair, then folded his arms over his chest as he looked up at the sky.

Opening the slider, she followed him outside. A lovely, cool breeze brushed against her skin. It was a beautiful early-July evening, and the stars twinkled like diamonds on black velvet. Beyond the patio there was a pool area with several wrought-iron chaises and chairs covered with thick pads for comfort.

She stood beside him, close enough to feel the warmth from his skin, but not touching. God help her if she touched him. "What is it, Luke?"

"You wouldn't understand."

"Try me. At least talk to me. Tell me what you're thinking."

"I'm mad as hell."

"That's a good start," she encouraged. "Why? I

thought hearing the terms of the estate would help. Are you angry with me?''

''Of course not. Why would you think that? You haven't kept anything from me.'' He looked at her, studied her gravely. ''Don't you see, Maddie? All I have are clues. Just hints that barely scratch the surface of who my father was.''

''Then I'm guessing you're upset with Flo and Tom.''

''Damn right I am. Their lie took away all my choices. If I had known, I might have wanted to meet him. I could have decided that I wanted to see what his personality was like. Get to know things about his health history. Am I anything like the guy whose DNA I carry?''

''I know that's upsetting—''

''No kidding. They should have told me and let me make the decision. Now I'll never know. The answers are dead and buried.''

''Not all of them,'' she said gently. ''Your parents have some of them. I'm sure they would be glad to tell you what they can.''

He turned to her, and the look in his eyes made her wince. ''What they can? That's the problem. Because they kept this from me, all I have are questions and no way to get *all* the answers.''

Madison couldn't stand by and watch him suffer so without trying to offer comfort. She moved half a step toward him and put her arms around his waist. He only hesitated a moment before drawing her closer, letting her rest her head on his chest. The next moment Madison wondered who was comforting whom.

She savored the solid, warm length of him. She reveled in his strength. She had never felt so safe and protected in her whole life. He held her for a long time, and she knew the precise moment his breathing changed, increased in rate.

"You smell like a meadow full of flowers," he said, his voice husky. "So clean and fresh and pure."

She lifted her head and met his gaze. In the moonlight she read the intensity there. It struck a wellspring within her, and her heart started pounding like a drum.

He rested his palm against her cheek, and she snuggled into the touch. His thumb gently, softly brushed across her lips as he looked at her, gauged her reaction, gave her the chance to stop him. She knew he was going to kiss her, but she couldn't find the will to protest.

He lowered his mouth to hers, and the contact sent a lightning bolt of pleasure arcing through her. He released her hair from the elastic scrunchy. Then his fingers threaded through her loose curls and cupped the back of her head, gently applying pressure that made the touch of their mouths more firm. With his tongue he traced the seam of her lips until the seductive movement encouraged her to open to him. Then he entered her, imitating the most intimate act between a man and a woman, and fire shot through her.

Madison felt the tingles that zinged from the top of her head to the soles of her feet, curling her toes, leaving her knees limp as linguine. If Luke hadn't been holding her, she would have fallen in a heap on the ground. But somehow she knew she could count on his strength. It was herself she didn't trust. Being this close to him was too much like coming home.

Especially when he moved his attention from her mouth to a sensitive spot just beneath her ear. When he concentrated there, she thought she would lose her mind. Like a rag doll, she stayed still and slack while he nibbled her ear, her jaw, her neck. The touch of his tongue, the warmth of his mouth, heated her blood and sent it singing through her veins. Her breasts swelled and her breathing grew labored, her willpower in shreds.

"We were good together, Maddie. Remember?" His voice was hoarse as he whispered in her ear.

"I remember."

She couldn't forget any more than she could resist him. If she could, she wouldn't be carrying his baby now. The thought sent a chill through her.

He lifted his head and met her gaze, his chest rising and falling rapidly. "It's July. You're not cold are you?"

She nodded and stepped away from him.

"It's warmer over here," he said with a roguish grin as he opened his arms. "I'm more than happy to share body heat."

And she was more than happy to let him. But she couldn't. "This is inappropriate."

"That's where you're wrong. Kissing you is the most appropriate thing I've done in a really long time."

She shook her head. "I can't, Luke. I'm sorry. It's all my fault. But I can't participate."

"Why?"

"We've been over this before. It's the reason I was reluctant to represent you."

"The suggestion of impropriety," he said, his voice tight with frustration.

"Yes. If I let it go on, it won't just be the suggestion. It will be a full-blown blooper." She folded her arms over her chest. "My career is important to me. I plan to make partner in the firm faster than anyone ever has—male or female."

"Is this for you? Or are you trying to prove something to someone? That you have a reason for being?"

There was a lot of truth in what he said. But she just didn't know how to answer him.

He rubbed the back of his neck. "Maddie, you don't have to prove anything to anyone. You're entitled to live your life the way you want. But have you thought through the goals you've set for yourself? Such a demanding career—"

"What do you mean?"

"You were made to have a family, children. What's that going to do to your career?"

Her stomach dropped to her toes. Did he know? How could he? It was time to tell him. She couldn't put it off any longer. He knew what was in the will. It would take time for him to deal with the ramifications. But she didn't have any time left. Here goes.

"Luke, there's something I need to tell you."

Chapter Six

In the moonlight Luke studied the serious expression on her face. "After what I've been through in the past couple of weeks, 'There's something I need to tell you' is not what I want to hear."

Maddie opened her mouth to respond, but the phone rang.

"Hold that thought," he said. Whatever she had to say couldn't be as life altering as finding out that he wasn't who he'd thought.

Luke went inside and picked up the phone in the kitchen. "Yeah?"

"Luke, this is Nick. Your big brother. Remember?"

Pain twisted through him at the reminder that he only had half a connection to this man he'd always looked up to and tried to emulate. At least now he understood why he'd always fallen short. They had different fathers.

"What's up, Nick?"

It had been on the tip of his tongue to call him what

was automatic after all these years, "Bro." But the word stuck in his throat.

"I need to talk to you."

"I have company." He glanced over his shoulder to find Maddie had followed him inside.

"I know. I'm on the cell phone and sitting in front of your house. We have to talk. But I didn't want to interrupt—"

"Okay. Maddie and I are finished, anyway. Give us a minute."

He hung up the phone and turned to her. "That was Nick."

"I heard."

"He's out front. Apparently what he needs to say can't wait. What did you want to tell me?"

"That *can* wait. It's time to mend fences with your brother." She gave him a wan look. "And don't start with the fractions. He's 100 percent your brother." She gathered up her paperwork and put it back in her briefcase. "Let me know when you want to discuss the estate in more detail. Your father's business is on automatic pilot for now. But sooner or later you're going to have to make some decisions."

"I'll call you."

She nodded. "Okay."

Luke noticed shadows in her green eyes. Again he had a feeling something was up with her. "Are you all right? Nick can wait if you want to talk."

She shook her head. "No. It will keep. Bond with Nick. We'll talk soon."

"Thanks for everything, Maddie."

"You're welcome."

He opened the door for her. "I'm not sorry about the kiss."

She met his gaze. "Neither am I," she said, then quickly walked down the steps. As she passed his brother she said, "Hi, Nick. Be gentle with him. Bye, Nick."

"I'll be as gentle as a middle linebacker. Bye, Maddie. Sorry to interrupt."

"No problem," she said over her shoulder. At the curb she got into her car and slammed the door shut.

Luke pulled his gaze from her fading taillights and focused on the angry features of his oldest half brother. Nick was three inches taller than him, with dark-brown eyes and hair. He was the CEO of Marchetti's Incorporated ever since Tom had retired. Right now he looked like one seriously angry first in command. In slacks, white shirt, and loosened, blue-striped tie, Luke guessed he'd come straight from the corporate offices.

He opened the door wider and held out his arm. "C'mon in. What can I do for you?"

Nick pulled a familiar envelope from his shirt pocket. "This is what you can do for me."

"My letter of resignation," Luke said, closing the door. "You didn't have to come in person to let me know you accept it."

"You should have delivered it in person."

"Why? There's nothing more to say."

"There's plenty to say." Nick's voice was a combination of anger and betrayal.

Luke felt bad about that. If anyone knew what betrayal felt like, it was him. He had just wanted to spare his brother the awkward conversation where he tried to be nice but was relieved that Luke was disappearing.

"I can't think of anything. Unless you don't know I have a different father."

"Mom and Dad told me. They told all of us."

"Rosie and Steve, too?"

"Yeah, your sister and her husband know. And guess what? We all think you've gone off the deep end."

Luke shrugged. They still stood in his empty living room. He recalled Maddie teasing him about it. God, he wished he'd asked her to stay for this. When she was with him, he never felt quite so adrift.

"Then everyone knows why I resigned," he said, ignoring the sarcastic comment.

Nick shook his head as he braced his feet wide apart and rested his hands on his hips. "You're going to have to explain that. I'm clueless and so is everyone else."

"It's simple. Marchetti's is a family-owned business. I'm not a member of the family." He shrugged. "I thought I would save you the time, aggravation and inconvenience of asking me to leave."

Nick laughed bitterly. "Dad always said you were the best and brightest. Boy, was he wrong."

He wasn't even Tom's son. Why would he say something like that? "What are you talking about?"

"You're dumb as a post if you think anything has changed. You're still my brother."

"*Half* brother," he clarified.

"We don't do the family thing in parts."

Luke recalled Maddie telling him the same thing, in different words. The corners of his mouth turned up at her phrasing. What part is still his brother? Hair, nose, hands, feet? But she wasn't walking in his shoes. Neither was Nick. They didn't know how it felt to discover your father wasn't who you'd always thought. She had called him exasperating. Had his biological father been that way, too? He would never know.

"Look, Nick, I appreciate the gesture. But it's not

necessary. I understand that I'm not a part of the business anymore. And I'm okay with it,'' he finished.

The words were a lie. It hurt like hell not to be involved with the business he'd been groomed to handle from the time he'd shown an aptitude for numbers. But he refused to hang around a venture he had no right to be a part of any longer. He wouldn't watch any feelings they might still have turn to annoyance and dislike. He couldn't stay where he wasn't wanted. He loved them all too much for that.

Nick shook his head in disgust. ''I can't believe we grew up together and I have to explain this to you. I love you. Joe, Alex and Rosie love you. Your niece and nephew love you. You promised that when they were old enough you would show them how to use those calculators you bought.''

''They've got their father and mother and two uncles. It doesn't take a mental giant,'' Luke ground out. That was a low blow, bringing the kids he would miss like crazy into this. ''You're not making this easy, Nick.''

''Good. I hope I'm making it damn hard. Mom and Dad are devastated about this,'' he said waving the letter.

''You don't need me.''

''That's where you're wrong,'' Nick said tightly. ''We all need you, professionally and personally. You owe them.''

Luke nodded. ''For a roof over my head, food on the table, clothes on my back and the best possible education.'' He let out a long breath. ''And they kept me from knowing who I am. What do you think that's worth?''

''Your thanks. Think about how much strength it took. They passed that on to you, Bro. This kind of news would have broken a weaker man. Thanks to Mom and

Dad, you're still on your feet." He held up the letter again. "This is your only slipup."

Luke ignored him. There was something else he needed to know. "How do you feel about Mom—knowing what she did?"

"I love her," Nick said simply. He raked a hand through his hair. "I know it's complicated. I try not to judge anyone unless I've walked in their shoes. I don't know what it's like to have three little kids and feel completely alone raising them. I'm not condoning her actions. But she's not a bad person. I'm trying to understand why it happened. I might have a better clue after Abby and I have our own baby. Bottom line—that's between her and Dad, and they dealt with it a long time ago."

Suddenly he took the letter in both hands and ripped it in two. Then he took the halves and tore them again and again until they were confetti-size.

"What did you do that for?" Luke asked.

"A gesture. Your resignation is denied, declined or whatever you want to call it."

"You have to accept it."

"No, I don't. We need you. And you need the job, especially now." For the first time since arriving, Nick smiled. "When were you two planning to break the news?"

"Two? Who? What are you talking about?"

"You and Maddie. The whole family knows you spent the night together after Alex and Fran got married. When were you going to tell us about the baby?"

Luke felt sucker-punched. "The baby?"

Oh, God. Was this what was up with Maddie?

"Yeah. Abby was in the obstetrician's waiting room for her monthly checkup and she saw Maddie there making an appointment for prenatal bloodwork. There was a reception area between them and the nurse had just called her back so she didn't get a chance to extend congratulations. So I'm doing it for both of us now. Congratulations, Luke,'' he said, holding out his hand.

Absently Luke took it. Maddie was going to have a baby? And she hadn't told him? Was there an epidemic of withholding information? Was there anyone he knew capable of telling him the truth? He damn well intended to find out.

Just a short time after leaving Luke, Madison walked out of her bathroom and leaned heavily against the wall as she heard her doorbell. ''Great. A visitor.''

She'd just tossed her lasagne and managed to brush her teeth. Her stomach felt better, but she'd never been more exhausted in her life. She pushed damp curls off her forehead and took a deep breath. It wasn't late, but she also wasn't expecting anyone. If she ignored whoever was there, maybe they would go away.

Her caller gave several long blasts on the bell. ''There's nothing worse than a persistent pest,'' she muttered, moving to respond.

Her stomach quivered when she peeked out the narrow window beside the door to see who was there. She opened up instantly. ''Luke! What's wrong?''

She wondered vaguely how she'd known so quickly that something was wrong. She certainly wasn't psychic, but she could deductive reason to beat the band. She'd only left him a short while ago with his brother and it was a good bet they'd had a confrontation. That and the thundercloud on his face spelled c-r-i-s-i-s.

''Why didn't you tell me you're pregnant?'' he

ground out. "Or maybe the appropriate question is—did you plan to ever tell me you're going to have my baby?"

Madison swayed unsteadily and grabbed on to the door for balance. "I...I don't know what to say. How did you find out?"

"You and Abby share a doctor. You didn't see her there?" he asked angrily.

Madison thought back and shook her head. "No."

The doctor's office was set up so that patients could leave the exam room, go down a corridor to the appointment desk and exit the office without having to go back through the waiting area. But there were opaque sliding doors on either side, and she guessed that Abby had seen her through there without Madison ever knowing. It wasn't a coincidence that she and Luke's sister-in-law had chosen the same one. The doctor was one of the best and came highly recommended. In fact, her practice was so busy Madison had at first been referred to someone else. She'd been accepted by promising to handle some legal issues for Dr. Virginia Olsen's pet project, a women's shelter.

"Come in, Luke. This isn't something I want to discuss on the porch." He walked in and she shut the door. "Can I get you a drink?"

"Yeah."

He followed her to the kitchen and rested his arms on the bar separating the refrigerator, stove and food-preparation area from the breakfast nook. Part of her was glad he kept his distance. The other part wished he would take her in his arms and hold her close to his solid body. She wanted him to tell her everything was going to be okay, even if it wasn't. But she'd never had anyone to lean on before. There was no reason to believe that would change now. More important, she couldn't afford to let him in, even for a little while. It would be too hard when he turned his back.

"Man, the lights just keep going off in my head," he said. "You're pregnant. That's why you were so adamant about no wine earlier."

She nodded as she pulled her step stool in front of the refrigerator. "And why I haven't had much of an appetite lately. And food doesn't always stay down." She climbed on the second step.

"What do you think you're doing?" he demanded.

"I'm getting you a drink," she explained. "I keep the scotch in the cupboard up there."

"I think not." He came around the bar and put his hands at her waist, easily lifting her off.

In spite of his high-handedness and the fact that he was angrier than she'd ever seen him, the gesture of protectiveness put a glow in her heart. Not to mention the heat that shot through her at the contact. Why couldn't she ignore him? Why did just a touch, or a look, or the barest hint of a smile from Luke Marchetti make her warm and weak and willing? Why did her heart beat faster when he held her just a little too long, a little too close?

Luke was a dead end. Even if she was relationship material, which she wasn't, his track record for settling down was nonexistent. To continue to experience any sensation in his presence, one would have to be a fool, a dreamer or both. Madison had strived from her earliest memory not to be either. She'd learned not to hope for what she wanted. The more she hoped, the harder and more painful the fall when she found out she wasn't enough to get it.

She shivered as he removed his hands from her waist. He then reached up to open the cupboard and lift down the bottle. It was a simple task, yet so masculine. And she wanted to sigh like a teenager with a heart-wrenching crush. She was putty in his hands. Or she would be if he touched her again. She'd proved that earlier when he'd kissed her. And how foolish had it been to tell him she wasn't sorry about it?

Backing up several steps, she watched him retrieve a tumbler and pour two fingers of the brown liquid into it. After capping the bottle, he tossed back the entire contents of the glass in two swallows. Then he sucked in a breath before grimacing slightly at the taste.

"Now where were we?" he asked. Before she could answer he said, "You were going to tell me about taking a page from the Flo and Tom Marchetti book of parenting and explain why you neglected to inform me that you're pregnant with my baby."

She shook her head, amazed at how he could be so sweet and tender one minute and go on the attack the next. He wasn't going to get away with it. She sympathized with what he was going through, and he had a point about her not telling him the news right away. But that didn't give him the right to be sarcastic and abrasive. The least he could do was listen.

"I don't especially like your attitude. And in case there's any doubt in your mind, listen up. You've used up your quota of sympathy from me. The martyr-victim syndrome will only carry you so far."

"Victim?" he asked, his voice deceptively calm compared to the fire in his eyes. "You'll be entitled to toss slings and arrows when you walk a mile in my loafers."

"Right back at you."

"Huh?"

"On more than one occasion you've told me that I don't know what you're going through. That no one understands. What was it you said earlier? Oh, yes. Do as I say not as I do.''

''What are you talking about?''

''You have no idea how I feel or what I'm going through. When you've got pregnancy hormones bebopping through your system then we can talk about the right way to handle doling out this kind of information. Until then, don't take that tone with me.'' She glared at him, her chest heaving. ''And if you'll recall, just before your brother showed up tonight, I told you I had to talk to you about something. I was going to tell you then.''

He nodded. ''What about all the other opportunities you had? You've obviously known for a while that you're pregnant.''

''I suspected right around the time I had to tell you your father wasn't who you'd always thought. I just couldn't say, 'You know your natural father? Well he isn't. And the guy who is, has passed away. Oh, and if all of that isn't bad enough, I'm carrying your baby.'''

''Not good enough, Maddie.''

Sometimes persistence was a positive character trait. Right now it just made her want to shake some sense into him. She studied his tall, muscular form and almost laughed at the idea of someone as small as she was shaking sense into a man practically twice her size.

''I did what I thought was best. Which, I might add, is what your parents did. I saw how the trauma rocked you and I just couldn't bear to burden you further. I wanted to give you some time to deal with that before I dropped this news on you, too.''

He shook his head. ''I should have known. When we were first together, you didn't think it was important to let me know you'd never been with a man.''

''What's that got to do with anything?''

"I should have known you were the type to hold back important information."

"There's holding back with intent to never divulge the information. Then there's picking and choosing an appropriate sensitive time to share the news."

"Semantics, just what I'd expect from you, Counselor."

She pulled air into her lungs as she brushed a strand of hair behind her ear. "Aside from the fact that I think you're being a stubborn, insensitive, obtuse, intractable jackass, there's one other thing that stopped me."

"And that would be?"

"You said in no uncertain terms that you didn't want children."

He froze and stared at her, shaking his head slightly. "I never said that."

"That's not something I'm likely to get wrong or make up, considering I'd just found out I was pregnant."

"When did I allegedly say that?" he demanded, moving toward her.

"The day you and Flo came to my office, when I gave you your father's letter. Just before your mother arrived, you were sitting in judgment of her, kind of like you are with me right now. I suggested that you might understand better if you had children of your own. You said, quite vehemently I might add, that you never wanted kids. I sure got a warm fuzzy from that."

He let out a long breath. "How would you feel in my position? How would you feel if the people you loved and trusted kept things from you? Really important things like who your father is?"

"If they cared about me, I would thank them. If I loved and trusted them, too, I would give them the benefit of the doubt. Trust that they believed they were doing the right thing.''

''You don't know—''

''You're right,'' she said. ''I don't know. But it's so easy to second-guess them now. I can tell you from personal experience that doing the wrong thing out of love is a darn sight better than being ignored.''

''Look, Maddie—''

''No, Luke. You look. I can't walk in your shoes, but I'm entitled to an opinion about it based on my own experiences. Did Flo and Tom send you away to boarding school while your siblings stayed at home and went to local private schools?''

''Of course not.''

''Were they conveniently out of the country when you graduated from high school, college and law school with honors?''

''I didn't go to law school,'' he said dryly.

''You know what I mean,'' she said huffily. ''Did they show up for commencement at the schools you did go to?''

''Yes.'' He looked at her. ''Calm down, Maddie. This can't be good for the baby.''

''Don't patronize me. Just answer the question.''

''Do you want me to state my name and swear on a Bible?''

She couldn't help a small smile as she said, ''The witness will please answer the question.''

''Just like my mother said, they were there from T-ball to cap and gown and everything in between. They demanded excellence and were there for the payoff.''

''You're lucky. My family didn't demand anything. I wasn't enough, could never do enough or be enough to get their attention.'' She let out a long breath. Suddenly she was almost too tired to stand. She slumped against the counter and rubbed a hand across her face. "Since nothing I say is good enough, this probably won't be, either. But here it is. I never lied to you, Luke."

"Not in so many words."

She sighed. "I planned to tell you about the baby. It should have been sooner, and I'm sorry you found out the way you did. But I was waiting until you had enough time to digest the news about your father. I was concerned that another bombshell would push you over the edge."

"You were worried about me? Afraid I might drive too fast?" He didn't quite smile.

"Silly me," she said, not actually confirming his question. And not denying it, either, since it was true.

"I'm tough, Maddie. I can take it."

"I'll remember that." She let out a long breath. "Now, I need to see you out. I'm really tired. I need to lie down before I fall down."

In a single stride he was beside her. Without a word he lifted her into his strong arms and started down the hall.

"What are you doing?" she asked, too weary to infuse her voice with the outrage she knew should be there.

She was just too darn grateful that she didn't have to walk. Too happy he was holding her. Too profoundly glad that he'd actually *listened* and really *heard* her. The people who should have cared about her never did. Did Luke care about her? Hardly. How could he? He thought she was a liar. Did she care about him? That was a no-brainer. The question: How *much* did she care and how could she stop?

She wished she could go back to the casual friendship

they'd shared before sleeping together. Somehow that intimacy had cracked the wall around her heart. Every time she saw him the crack grew wider until she feared he would take possession of her soul. She couldn't let that happen. It would be too desolate if she knew he couldn't return her feelings.

"Your stomach is growling," he said, a smile in his voice.

"Don't tell Alex and Fran, but their designer frozen entrée didn't stay down."

"I think they would understand," he said. "But it will be our secret."

He placed her very gently on her bed. With his hands on either side of her, neatly pinning her, he met her gaze with the same intensity that always stole the breath from her lungs. "I need to feed you—again," he said.

When he straightened, she made a great show of settling herself in a half-reclining position with pillows at her back. She needed to do something to keep him from noticing how profoundly his nearness affected her. After all, they had returned to the scene of the crime.

"I don't feel much like eating," she answered.

"There's a rumor that pregnant women have cravings. Is there something that sounds good?"

"The doctor said I need to have a lot of protein."

"How about a steak?"

She shuddered at the suggestion. After a moment's thought she said, "It's really high in fat, but peanut butter and jelly sounds like heaven."

"I'll make you a sandwich."

"That's sweet of you, but I don't have any."

He looked her over from head to toe and the intensity in his gaze made her skin tingle. "I'm no doctor, but in my opinion you could use a little fat. I'll go to the market.'' He started for the doorway and half turned. ''Smooth or crunchy?''

''What?''

''Peanut butter. Do you like smooth or the kind that's mostly peanuts with token smooth thrown in?''

''I'm a superchunk kind of girl.''

One corner of his mouth turned up. ''Yeah. I kind of figured that.''

Then he was gone. And, God help her, she missed him. The him who was sweet and kind. *And* the one who was confrontational and angry. She missed all of him, even though she had a hunch this was the calm before the storm. Her life felt like a dresser drawer pulled out and dumped on the floor. If anyone knew how she felt it was Luke. He'd gotten the double whammy. And they hadn't settled anything. But he was coming back with peanut butter. How sweet was that?

There was no question in her mind. Life as she'd known it was about to change.

Chapter Seven

Madison put her key in her front door, then let out a startled squeal as a dark figure materialized from the shadows on her porch.

"Luke!" She pressed a hand to her chest, as if that would control her pounding heart. "What are you doing here?"

"It's late, Maddie," he said, ignoring her question. "Keeping hours like this can't be good for the baby."

"Neither is scaring the life out of the baby's mother. What are you doing here?" she asked again.

A rhetorical question, she realized. She knew why he was there. Several days had passed since he'd found out she was pregnant. Several days during which it hadn't been far from her mind that he'd served her a peanut butter and jelly sandwich and a glass of milk on a tray while she'd rested in the bed where they'd conceived their baby. He'd stayed with her to make sure she consumed every last crumb of food and drop of milk, then had told her to get some sleep. They could talk the following day.

He rested a hand on the door frame and looked down at her. "I've tried to reach you for three days. I've left messages everywhere. The evidence would suggest you're avoiding me. Why?"

"I had a doctor's appointment. Prenatal bloodwork," she said, extending her arm so he could see the gauze and Band-Aid on the inside of her elbow.

Her action had nothing to do with proving to him that she was telling him the truth. It was all about keeping him from noticing that she'd deflected the other part of his question which was why she'd been avoiding him. She should have known a man of action like Luke would just show up on her doorstep.

He took her forearm in his large hand as he inspected her wound. Too late she realized her error in judgment to let him see, but she hadn't figured on his touch. With his index finger, he stroked the tender, sensitive flesh of her inner wrist. Tingles raced over her skin, up her arm, settling in her breasts. *This* was why she'd been avoiding him. He did things to her, inside and out, that scared her. Her feelings were new, strange, and so big they frightened her.

He didn't have much respect for her; he'd made that abundantly clear. How could anything lasting and satisfying grow out of that? It would be stupid to hope for anything, even if she wanted it. And instinctively she knew that he could hurt her as no one else ever had— or ever could.

"You should have told me about the appointment," he gently scolded in a deep, seductive voice that raised gooseflesh on her arms and kicked up her breathing. "I needed to be there," he said.

She pulled her hand away from his touch. "Why? No one needs to document *your* weight, do *your* bloodwork, or take *your* blood pressure. Although, judging by the look on your face, a date with the blood-pressure cuff isn't such a bad idea."

"Can you blame me? This baby is mine, too. I want to know everything that's going on."

"So you've changed your mind about wanting kids?" she asked, challenging him.

Madison hadn't realized how important his answer would be until she'd asked the question. When she'd reminded him, he hadn't denied the truth of his comment about not wanting children. He'd only made excuses for saying it. She would never have chosen these circumstances for bringing a child into the world. In fact, based on her own less-than-ideal childhood, she would never have made the choice to conceive. If children learned what they lived, she'd learned to be distant and uninvolved. She'd had no role model for being Mother Earth incarnate. But now that she was facing the possibility, she found she very much wanted this baby. Did Luke? She planned to love this child with every ounce of her being. Could Luke?

In hindsight she realized another reason she'd put off telling him about the baby was because she couldn't bear to hear that he didn't want it.

He ran a hand through his hair, then crossed his arms over his chest. "It's my right to be involved in the decisions regarding this child," was all he said.

"I see," she answered. But it felt like a giant fist was squeezing the life from her heart. That wasn't at all what she'd hoped to hear.

She opened her door, reaching in to flip two switches, one for the porch light, the other to illuminate the living room of her condo. Then she met Luke's gaze and heaved a tired sigh. The memory of him carrying her to the bedroom the last time he'd been here flashed through her mind. On the heels of that recollection was a burst of warmth and tenderness for this man.

But his answer didn't reassure her that he'd changed his mind about wanting children.

She stood in the doorway. In spite of herself, her heart went out to him, the dark confusion in his eyes, the frown on his face. "I'll raise this baby on my own and let you know if anything comes up that we need to discuss. Good night." She started to close the door.

He put his palm on it, effectively stopping her. "Not so fast. Based on your behavior patterns, why should I believe you'll keep me informed?"

She put her hand on her hip, and met his gaze. "And what behavior pattern would that be?"

"The one where you hold back important information that I'm entitled to have."

"How quickly they forget," she mumbled. "Whatever happened to 'innocent until proven guilty'? You accused me of lying about your father, and found out you were wrong. And technically I didn't hold back information about the baby. You found out from someone else before I had a chance to tell you."

"You had numerous opportunities and chose not to tell me. I'll never know for sure whether or not you planned to inform me that I'm going to be a father."

"And I have no way of proving that I was waiting for the right time. Take it from an attorney, conspiracy is one of the toughest things to prove in court." She stared at him, wanting to clobber him and kiss him and cuddle into his warm strength all at the same time. "So where does that leave us?"

"It leaves us at a place where I think we should get married."

"Married?" She blinked and studied his features. There wasn't a hint of a smile. No mischievous twinkle in his eyes. No cute, quirky curling of his mouth indicating that he was kidding. No flash of dimples. And how she wished there was all of the above. "You're not serious."

"I've never been more serious about anything in my life," he replied.

Luke realized it was true. He hadn't planned to blurt out a proposal that way. But now that he had, he knew it was the right thing to do. He'd spent the better part of his adult life looking for Ms. Right without success. He wanted to do what his brothers and sister had: settle down with one person. But he hadn't met the woman who rang his chimes, set off the bells and whistles, made him see fireworks. He had reached the point where he believed it was time to settle—period—for whatever woman seemed to meet most of his criteria.

Then he'd kissed Maddie. The fire she'd kindled in him incinerated any imagined list of qualifications. Then came an even bigger shock. She'd been a virgin. She'd let him be her first. He'd begun to hope she was the one. It had thrown him for a loop when he'd found out, first, that he couldn't trust his parents, then that he couldn't believe in her. In spite of that, he couldn't seem to control his attraction for her. He thought about her all hours of the day and night. He wanted to be with her, even though he knew sooner or later this need for her would fade.

Math had taught him the accuracy of pattern. Typically he felt instant fascination for a woman that fairly quickly died out. For reasons he couldn't explain, Maddie's appeal had grown over time. It was even stronger now. But based on his past history, it would disappear. He'd been prepared to settle for someone. Why not with the woman who was carrying his child?

"I think you'd better come inside," she said with a sigh. Standing back, she opened the door wider. "We seem to have established a bad habit of discussing monumental occurrences on my doorstep."

"Okay." He suppressed a smile. How did she do that? His whole life was in the dumper and she could make him want to grin.

He walked past her, inhaling the sweet, flowery scent of her perfume. If he lost his sight tomorrow, he knew he could find his way to Maddie by the fragrance that was hers alone. It burrowed inside him and imprinted on his mind.

She set her briefcase down by the beige love seat. Unlike his place, her living room was completely furnished. Floral throw pillows in green, beige and peach floral fabric that matched the chair and ottoman rested on the couch. Mahogany coffee and end tables and various knickknacks completed the cozy conversation area.

"Have you eaten dinner?" she asked.

He shook his head. "More important—have you?"

"I was about to fix a peanut butter sandwich," she answered. "It seems to be the magic recipe. Would you like one?"

He couldn't hold back the grin any longer. "Sure."

She kicked off her high heels, and in stocking feet walked to the kitchen. Barefoot and pregnant. In a calf-length, tailored linen dress, she almost looked like she was playing dress-up with her mother's clothes. She looked so small, so fragile. She made him want to protect her, take care of her. And need her? No. He couldn't get their one night of unbridled passion out of his mind. It was probably the best night of his life. But need her? No way. He would never need her or anyone else again.

Pulling bread, peanut butter and jelly and paper plates from the cupboards, she started fixing sandwiches. Then she garnished each with pieces of apple and raw carrots.

She set the plates on the kitchen table and poured two glasses of milk. "Voilà. A well-balanced meal."

"What if I said it wasn't hot?"

"I'd call you names like fussy, hoity-toity, snob, then I'd toast yours," she said, sitting down with a sigh.

He sat down at a right angle to her and took a bite of half his sandwich. He liked that she'd cut them in triangles. His mother had always done that. But he didn't want to remember that time of absolute faith and innocence when he'd trusted without question. Instead, he turned his thoughts back to Maddie—and his marriage proposal.

"So what do you think?" he asked. "About getting married."

"Why should we?"

There was the sixty-four-thousand-dollar question. It was fairly complicated. Because Maddie was glib and quick-witted, he decided to keep his answer simple and unimpeachable. "Because it would be best for the baby."

She chewed thoughtfully, giving no clue about what she was thinking. "You know, it's been a long time since prospective parents who weren't married felt any obligation to get married merely for the sake of the unborn child."

"Is that a yes or no?" he asked.

"Neither. It's a statement of fact."

"Is there a yes or no anywhere in my immediate future?" he asked.

"No."

"No you don't have an answer? Or no on getting married?"

"No on marriage," she said. "Although it's very noble of you to ask."

Semi-stunned, he waited for her to elaborate. When she didn't, he said, "Do you want to tell me why?"

"It's a new millennium. Women are no longer obligated to marry just because they're having a baby without benefit of marriage."

"What about your position at the law firm? Won't this affect your run on a partnership? You've been spouting legalese to me for weeks. As far as impropriety goes, this is right up there."

"Not anymore. Women are single-parenting all the time in this day and age," she said. "And in the firm, precedent has already been set. One of the senior partners is a woman who also happens to be a single mother and never married her baby's father. This decision won't affect my upward mobility. I can still make partner faster than anyone has. My clients don't care about my situation. Their only concern is the best possible legal counsel. I can give them that. Thank you for your offer, but I have to respectfully decline."

"But marriage is the next logical step," he countered.

At least to him it was. She'd hesitated to tell him about the baby because of his remark about not wanting kids. And he'd told her he wanted to be in on the decisions. That didn't scratch the surface of how he felt about becoming a father. But right now, all he knew for sure was that he didn't want his child to ever wonder about who his father was and where he fit.

"Marriage is the only way to ensure that I will be involved in my child's life."

"Marriage doesn't guarantee anything. Believe me, as a lawyer, I know. But I would never deprive you of your child. You're going to have to take my word for that."

"All evidence to the contrary," he countered.

"I have never lied to you." Her green eyes flashed annoyance. "How long are you going to punish me for waiting to give you more news that would rock your world? How long am I going to pay for being sensitive to what you were going through?"

"I'm not punishing you. Just being practical."

"For the last time, I'll admit it was wrong to wait. I will regret for the rest of my life that you found out the news from someone else. In my own defense, my heart was in the right place. I held back for the right reason."

"Getting married for the baby is the right reason."

She shook her head. "Arguably, it's the right thing. But it is motivated by the wrong reason."

"Is it because I'm not a Marchetti?"

He'd asked her once before if she refused to handle his legal affairs because he wasn't a Marchetti, and she'd denied it, then called him exasperating. But he also knew how much she liked the big Marchetti family. She'd once told him that was something she'd never had. Now that he was no longer one of them, maybe that was why she wanted nothing to do with him.

She cocked her head to the side and studied him. "It's comforting to know that some things don't change. You're still exasperating. But here's the bottom line—I won't marry a man who's made it clear that he doesn't trust me. Without that, there can't be love, which is the only right reason to get married."

He didn't believe in love. In all these years, it hadn't

happened to him, and he had no reason to think that would change. But her refusal rankled. Getting married was right—for the baby, he added to himself. "Is that your final answer?"

"Yes."

If he'd never discovered his parent's lie, he would never have questioned her timing in telling him about the pregnancy. He knew he should let it go and give her the benefit of the doubt. But he couldn't seem to. He hated that the two people who had been his foundation, were now responsible for his doubts. He hated that he'd been made a fool of—twice.

He studied Maddie. How could she so calmly turn him down and finish her milk? When she set the glass beside her empty paper plate, he wanted to kiss the white mustache from her upper lip. When she licked it off herself, he went hot and hard. He wanted her—here and now. How could his feelings for this woman swing so drastically from one end of the spectrum to the other?

Why?

She'd refused to marry him. Still he wanted her. In spite of everything. He had a bad feeling that the same woman he couldn't trust was the one he wouldn't be able to forget. The whole thing confused the hell out of him, so he decided to put it out of his mind. Instead he focused on a more immediate problem.

Since she wouldn't marry him, how was he going to watch over her and the baby?

It was almost eight o'clock in the evening when Madison lugged the first of several bags of groceries into her kitchen through the door to her garage. The doctor had stressed the importance of a well-balanced diet to nourish the baby. However, keeping fresh fruits, vegetables, protein and dairy on hand was going to consume a good portion of her time at the grocery store. Between her job and the pro bono work she was doing for the women's shelter, she didn't have a lot of time to spare. At least it kept her too busy to think about Luke. During the day.

The nights were a different story. When she turned off the light and closed her eyes, his face was there. The mental picture created an almost physical pain inside her. When would she get over this strange urgency to have his arms around her? If she'd never experienced the incredibly wonderful sensation, would her yearning be so fierce? Although they had talked on the phone, she hadn't seen him in a few weeks. The more time that passed, the bigger the ache.

As perverse as it sounded, she'd sort of hoped he wouldn't give up on her. And she'd begun to suspect he had. She ignored the tight sensation in her chest at the thought.

As she started back to the garage for another bag, her doorbell rang. Annoyed, she shook her head. ''If that's a salesman, he's going to rue the day he rang my chimes,'' she grumbled as she walked through the living room.

When she answered the door, Luke Marchetti stood there. Definitely not a salesman, unless he was still hawking wedding vows. But once upon a time he'd definitely rung her chimes.

He held up a measuring cup. ''Can I borrow some sugar, sugar?''

''Don't call me sugar,'' she said absently.

She blinked several times, wondering if her thoughts had conjured him up. He looked good, leaning against her door frame, decidedly pleased about something. He was wearing worn jeans, a T-shirt that hugged his biceps, and it looked as if he'd been in a hurry when he stuck his bare feet, without socks, into deck shoes. The corners of his mouth turned up, showing off his dynamite dimples to perfection. But it was the look in his eyes that took her breath away. His gaze seemed to drink in the sight of her, as if he might have missed her, as if he wanted to consume her. Suddenly flutters replaced that tight feeling in her chest, and tingles skittered down her arms.

How in the world was she supposed to resist this man?

Then his words sank in. "Borrow a cup of sugar?" she asked. "Don't you have neighbors for that?"

"I do now," he said with a grin that turned her knees the consistency of ice cream left out in the sun too long. He cocked his thumb toward the unit next to hers. "I moved in next door to you this morning."

"What are you talking about? I didn't know the place was up for sale."

"It wasn't. I made an offer they couldn't refuse."

"There hasn't been enough time to close an escrow. It must have been some offer."

He grinned. "I'm renting back from them until the paperwork clears. And it was a generous offer. My lawyer informed me that I've inherited a lot of money. I can do anything I want. Especially since I have motive and means."

"Motive?"

"You won't marry me, and I want to be around for the baby."

When he shrugged one broad, masculine shoulder, Madison's mouth went dry. Why did he have to do that? Why couldn't he manage to be a little less masculine? It would be so much easier on her. But, no. He could be the world-renowned spokesman for macho. And as if that weren't enough, there was that small tuft of chest hair that just barely curled over the top of his T-shirt. It made her want to slide her palms up under the material, run her hands over the bare muscular contours and...

This was crazy. This way he had of distracting her. Surely he wasn't serious about living next door to her.

"You're pulling my leg," she said.

He made a cross over his heart, on that mouth-watering chest. "On my honor, I'm telling the truth."

"Then you're spying on me."

"*Spy* is such a harsh word."

"True nonetheless, since you didn't bother to deny it."

She flinched, then a delicious shiver skipped over her when he shrugged again. A distraction. Something to blunt the force of his incredible appeal was what she desperately needed. "Look, can we talk about this another time? I've got bags of groceries still in the car. I'll assimilate my feelings, then—"

He walked past her through her living room. Over his shoulder he said, "I'll get the bags out of the car. You shouldn't be carrying them in your condition."

"Wait a minute. I didn't invite you in. I haven't decided how I feel about your underhandedness," she said, hurrying after him like a passenger who'd just missed the train by seconds.

He'd disappeared when she reached the kitchen. A moment later she heard her trunk slam shut. Then he reappeared with the remainder of her groceries, carrying them in one hand. It would have taken her three trips, on tired legs that wanted to be elevated. She had to admit she was glad he'd been there. But she would only admit it to herself. And only for a split second. It felt too good not to come home to an empty condo, and she didn't want to get used to it. As soon as he realized she wasn't someone he could care about, he would be gone. And she wouldn't blame him.

"I didn't hear what you said," he commented, pulling milk, eggs and lettuce out of one bag.

"I said you're an underhanded sneak. Why didn't you tell me you were moving in next door?"

"I didn't want to get your hopes up until I was sure the deal would go through."

She unloaded her bag of potatoes into the bin in the pantry. "You are the most arrogant man. It couldn't possibly have anything to do with the fact that you were afraid I'd clobber you. This withholding of information?"

He narrowed his gaze on her. "Are you angry?" he asked, not responding to her accusation.

She stood by the island, absently taking grocery items out of the bags. "Angry, annoyed, aggravated, agitated."

"All those negative A words can't be good for the baby. Or are you just showing off your vocabulary?"

She smiled. She wasn't sure how she felt, except that it was wonderful to see him. And she was annoyed that it was so wonderful. But he was looking more relaxed than she'd seen him in a long time. Probably because of the baby, she reminded herself. Was it possible he wanted this child? At least it took his mind off what he was going through with his parents. But that was the only reason he was here. She must never, ever make the mistake of believing it was about her, no matter how much she might want to.

"I'm not exactly sure how I feel about this," she admitted. "When I figure it out, you'll probably hear the explosion and smell the smoke, especially now that you're so close," she said wryly.

"If I hadn't been here, unloading these groceries would have taken you twice as long," he said, wadding up the last bag and throwing it in the trash.

"Counsel will so stipulate. A strong back does come in handy." Her heart skipped a beat when he grinned.

"Okay, hide behind legal double-talk if you have to. But you and I both know the truth."

"And what's that?" she asked, praying he hadn't a clue.

"Having me around will be a good thing. I can fetch, carry, cook a mean peanut butter sandwich and assemble anything that you might need assembled. I'm a pro bono handyman. Just pound on the wall and I can be here in a heartbeat."

Madison glanced at the wall separating her unit from his. She prayed it was thicker than she thought. One flimsy wall between them. It wasn't nearly enough.

More important, there was something she needed to make him believe. "This is the last time I'm going to bring this up, Luke. But I want to put it out there.... You said you want to have a say in all the decisions regarding our baby. I respect that, and I'm glad you want to be included. I would never keep this child from you."

"If you say so, Maddie."

So much for making him believe. Still, considering what he was dealing with regarding his family, she could hardly blame him. But she had bigger fish to fry. Like how she was going to resist him right next door when her libido got the better of her.

That told her instantly how she felt about his close living quarters. Scared with a capital *S*. Would that flimsy plaster-and-wood barrier be enough? It had to be. No way would he care about her.

But she had an awful feeling that if she let herself care for Luke, unbelievable pain and devastation would follow. She couldn't let that happen.

She'd meant what she'd said about including him in the baby's life. But hers was strictly off-limits to him.

Chapter Eight

The day after carrying Maddie's groceries, Luke was loading some boxes from his old place into the back of his car. Manual labor had been good to take his mind off the chaos in his life, but he admitted it was losing some appeal.

Just then a familiar vehicle pulled up behind his. When he saw Joe, Alex and Rosie get out, he knew why. He also recognized they had their stubborn faces on. He recalled the bet he'd made with Maddie about convincing his siblings that he was no longer a member of the family, and knew that reinforcements had arrived and his uphill battle was about to commence.

The three of them walked toward him, and he braced himself, resting his back against the car as he crossed his arms over his chest.

"Hey," he said. "What are you guys doing here?"

Rosie's dark eyes narrowed, and her curly dark hair blew in the breeze as she put her hands on her hips. "So many bones to pick with you, so little time," she said, shaking her head. "For starters, we're here to tell you what a blockhead you are."

"Don't sugarcoat it, Ro. Tell me how you really feel." He looked at the others and made a show of counting heads. "Three. Someone's missing? Where's Nick?"

Alex cleared his throat. He had the brown eyes and wavy dark hair all the Marchettis shared but was more slender than Joe. "We tried to get Nick to back us up, but he refused to waste his breath again. He told us he tore up your letter of resignation and said to tell you from him that you're a stubborn jackass. A moron. An idiot."

"If you guys came to call me names—" he shrugged "—maybe we should go inside."

"Yeah," Joe said. "We wouldn't want your neighbors to know what a dolt, a dunce—"

"Enough. I get the message." Luke led the way up the sidewalk.

Joe was right behind him. His coloring was the same as the others, but his body type was a little different, more like a football player. "We want to know when you're going to quit pouting and come back to work."

"I will not admit to the pouting part. As far as coming back to work? I don't know that I am," Luke admitted, holding the door open for them.

"Ever?" Joe asked, astonishment in his voice. They entered the unfurnished living room that now had boxes scattered around. "You can't mean that."

"On the contrary. My lawyer has informed me that my father left me a sizable inheritance along with a profitable business."

"But we're family," Rosie protested.

"Only half," Luke clarified. "Mom's half. Dad—

Tom—built the business for you guys. Under the circumstances, I think it would be easier if I walk away.''

Alex stood beside Rosie and folded his arms over his chest. ''Don't you think you should talk to Dad and let him make the decision?''

''I think if I do it quietly, it will save everyone the time, trouble and awkwardness of easing me out.''

''What makes you think we want you out?'' Alex demanded. ''Have we indicated by word or deed that we feel any differently about you? You're the same stubborn, opinionated, hardhead we know and love.''

Angrily Rosie tossed a long strand of hair over her shoulder. ''Years of bonding don't disappear just because you found out your biological father is someone else. Mom and Dad opened their arms and hearts to my husband, Steve, when he was just a mixed-up kid. They treated him like a son. But you *are* their son. They love you. We love you. You're part of this family as much as any of us. Nothing can change that.''

''Something did. The fact that our mother had an affair and I'm the result,'' Luke said angrily.

''I knew the folks had problems at one time,'' Joe admitted. He looked down for a moment, then met his gaze. ''Ma told me about it when I was having trouble making a commitment to Liz. All my friends seemed to be splitting up and there was a childhood memory I couldn't put to rest. It was the only time I saw Ma cry.''

''What did she tell you?'' Luke asked.

''That she was unfaithful. They split up. I was the only one who saw her cry when Dad left, and it stayed with me. For years I went on about how they'd had a perfect marriage, but refused to let myself fall in love. After Ma and I talked, I got past it. Thanks to her, Liz and I resolved our differences and couldn't be happier now.''

"And you didn't see fit to tell the rest of us?" Luke demanded.

"Ma gave me her permission, but I didn't see the point of rehashing it, embarrassing her," Joe explained.

"So she stopped short of telling you I was the result of her infidelity?" Luke said, his gut twisting with anger because he'd had the props knocked out from under him.

"She was protecting you, not herself. And if she had filled me in, it wouldn't change the way I feel about you. The way we all feel about you," he said, glancing at Alex and their sister who were nodding. "Or the way the folks feel about you."

Luke studied their faces and could see nothing but sincerity in the familiar features. "It doesn't bother you that they kept the truth from all of us?"

Rosie sighed. "I have two children. If I didn't, it might be hard, maybe downright impossible to understand why they kept this to themselves. But I can see that they were giving you a safe, secure life. It's what parents who love their children do. Ma told me no one was ever supposed to find out. They'd agreed to keep it secret for your sake."

"And no one else thinks that's wrong?" he asked, searching their faces for a sign that they agreed with him.

Rosie met his gaze. "How would you have felt as a child knowing this? For Pete's sake, you're a grown man now and having difficulty with it. I'd go so far as to say you're behaving like a child. And I have to tell you, Luke, it's pretty unattractive."

In spite of his churning feelings, the corners of his mouth turned up. Leave it to Rosie to tell it like it was.

Not unlike the pretty redhead he couldn't seem to get out of his mind. Maddie. He couldn't wait to see her again. In fact, now that he lived next door to her, the phrase "so near, yet so far" had new meaning for him.

"I haven't made a final decision about work yet," he said, changing the subject. "But I don't want to keep you hanging. You've got a business to run."

"*We've* got a business to run," Joe said. "As the human resources director I can tell you to take all the time you need to think this through. Although I can save you time and effort. The right decision is to come back to work with us."

"If you don't care about us, think about your baby," Rosie said.

"You guys know?" Luke asked, surprised.

Feigning exasperation, Alex shook his head. "I can't understand how you could grow up in this family and act amazed when the meddling Marchettis behave true to form. Of course we know. We all know you and Maddie spent the night together after my wedding. We all know Abby saw her at the obstetrician making another appointment. It's not a big leap to make the connection that she's carrying your baby."

Luke rubbed a hand across his face. "If we're talking about true to character, you all probably knew before I did. Maddie kept me in the dark. I can't say for sure that she was ever going to clue me in."

"Of course she was," Rosie said confidently. "She was just waiting for a good time to spring the news on you. In her shoes, considering what you were going through, all of us would have held off telling you about becoming a mother."

Joe cleared his throat. "Don't look now, Sis, but since

I'm biologically incapable of being a mother, I would have nothing to hold off about.''

Rosie slugged him playfully, and Luke felt as if he was the one who took a punch. He hadn't realized until seeing them—the playfulness, the support, the caring—how much he'd missed his brothers and sister. They were so much a part of his life and always had been. Could he trust that they were sincere about their feelings? That his different DNA strand made no difference in the way they felt about him?

As if she could read his thoughts, Rosie moved to Luke's side and put her hand through the crook of his elbow, then rested her head against his shoulder for a moment.

''As I have been so rudely and insensitively reminded, none of you bozos can understand what raging hormones feel like,'' she said. ''But *I* can sympathize with Maddie. She was the one who had the unenviable task of telling you about your father. In her shoes I would have waited to spring the news about a baby. You need to stop taking it out on her that your father isn't who you thought he was.''

''Rosie's right, Luke,'' Alex said. ''Given the same circumstances, I probably would have done the same thing. You can't hold it against her that Nick was the one who broke the news. Give her the benefit of the doubt. You know you would have if it wasn't for all this other stuff.''

Luke had thought the same thing himself. But his world was rocked. He didn't know who he was. How could he know what he would have done? Now that he knew the full significance of having vital information withheld, it was damn hard to brush off something as important as not telling him she was pregnant with his child.

He covered Rosie's hand with his own. "You're all going to jump down my throat, but none of you knows what it feels like to walk in my shoes."

Joe folded his arms over his chest. "Maybe not. But I know you pretty well, Bro. And I'd bet that you want what the rest of us have."

"Which is?"

Rosie looked up at him. "Someone special and a family," she said simply.

Alex stuck his fingertips in the pockets of his slacks. "I know you don't want to hear that Ma is right about anything, but we all agree with her about this. You and Maddie are perfect for each other."

Luke laughed. "You couldn't be more wrong."

Rosie squeezed his arm and gave him a dazzling smile. "Atta boy. Words to warm a meddler's heart. You have absolutely convinced me that you and Maddie are a match made in heaven."

"You guys are a bunch of incurable, hopeless romantics. Ma has you all brainwashed," Luke said, shaking his head.

"When you can find it in you to forgive her," Joe said, "you'll see that Ma's right when it comes to matters of the heart. And she and Dad have done a damn fine job raising us, including you."

Luke put a hand over his shirt pocket, making sure the letter his biological father had left him was still there and not misplaced in the move. He wasn't convinced that he could ever forgive his mother for deceiving him about something as basic as who he was. But talking to his siblings had somehow lightened his heart. He'd missed them. He was grateful to them for stopping by to call him names. Nothing else could have convinced him more completely that they still felt the same about him.

Rosie gave his arm a quick hug, then let him go and looked around at the boxes. "So do you want to tell us what's going on?"

"I'm moving into the condo next to Maddie's."

Joe gave him a look that said if he was any dumber, he couldn't be trusted by himself. "Wouldn't it be simpler to move in *with* the mother of your child? And here's a wild idea—marry her?"

"I already tried that. She turned me down."

Rosie clasped her hands together and grinned like a fool. "I knew it. Like I said, perfect for each other."

"Sis," Luke countered, "I think you should talk to someone about this unrealistic romantic streak of yours."

She pointed at him. "I'll talk to *you* at your wedding to Maddie. Now, I don't know about you guys, but I have to get back to my children and my bookstore." She glanced at Joe and Alex, who nodded. "I think our work here is done."

Luke grinned at them. "I promise to think about everything you said."

"What we said about the job? Or Maddie?" Joe asked.

"Both," Luke promised. Then he hugged each of his siblings in turn and watched them as they walked to the car. Just before climbing in the front seat, Rosie looked at him and ran back.

"There's one more thing, Luke."

"What?"

"Dad was going to come with us today. Then he changed his mind. He said this was a sibling thing. But he wanted me to tell you that he'll talk to you soon. When you're ready.''

Luke nodded, not sure how he felt about that. ''Okay.''

She stood on tiptoe and kissed his cheek. ''I love you.''

Then she ran back to the car and slid into the front seat. As they honked and drove away, Luke returned their wave.

Remembering his promise to think about Maddie and the job, he decided thinking about her was easier, as simple as falling off a log. Never had a woman so profoundly and thoroughly captured his mind. The thought caught him up short.

Okay, he would admit that she popped into his mind more than he was comfortable with. But capture his heart? No woman ever had. So how could Maddie accomplish that impossible feat? Especially when he wasn't altogether certain he could trust her?

After a Saturday shopping trip, Madison pulled into her garage and saw Luke beside it. Was he waiting for her? God help her, she was happy to see him. Then she remembered that as of the day before, he lived next door. It wasn't a stretch for her to run into him. Oddly enough, since he'd dropped by to borrow sugar after moving, she hadn't been able to work up more than a token mad at him for his aggressive high-handedness.

Why?

Together she and Luke had created this ''accident'' she was carrying. So she could understand an unplanned pregnancy. But attitude about the blessed event made all the difference. Unlike her mother and father, she found she desperately wanted this child. But she didn't think either that or hormones explained why she had cut Luke some slack for his overly aggressive behavior.

She'd accused him of spying on her. But he'd also proposed marriage. When she turned him down, he'd taken up residence next door to watch over her and the baby. That amounted to more commitment than she'd ever felt from her parents. Which was probably why she hadn't been able to sustain any sincere anger toward him.

It had always seemed to her that her mother and father just couldn't be bothered with a little girl they hadn't wanted. As long as there was breath in her body, this baby would never feel like a nonessential entity. But she was afraid Luke's actions were more about acting out his feelings concerning not knowing his own biological father. He needed to feel he was in control.

His spontaneous kindness could never be about tender, reciprocal feelings toward her. She refused to waste time and energy on hope that Luke could be different. If her own flesh and blood couldn't love her, why should he?

She opened her car door and got out, walking over to him. "Waiting for me? Don't even bother to tell me you just arrived."

His lips curved into a small smile, unleashing dimples that should be registered with the love police as a dangerous weapon. "Okay, I won't tell you that. Even though it's the truth. Let's just say I'm here to pay up on our bet."

"What bet?"

"The one where you wagered that my siblings wouldn't let me go quietly." He reached in his pocket, pulled out some folded bills and handed her a twenty.

She took it, carefully avoiding the warmth of his fingers. "What happened?"

"Joe, Alex and Rosie came to see me. And now I need you to put on your attorney hat."

She put her key in her trunk and opened it. Then she tipped her head to the side. "I think this whole neighbor thing is less about borrowing sugar and more about a cup of free legal advice."

"You can bill me if you want."

"Okay. I'll save a stamp and slip it under your door."

He peeked in her trunk. "You've been shopping."

Was that disapproval in his tone? "Before you start in on me, buying a crib is technically not a decision about the baby that I felt warranted input from the baby's father."

"You're still trying to keep me at arm's length."

"I fail to see how or why you would be miffed. Most men would kiss my feet for letting them off the hook on a shopping trip."

"I'm not most men. And while I would gladly kiss your feet, or any and all other parts of you, you're deliberately missing my point. Picking out a baby's bed is an experience intimate to prospective parents. It's something that brings them closer. You intentionally left me out. Why, Maddie? What are you afraid of?"

She was too busy reeling from his admission that he wanted to kiss her all over. The seductive visual sent a surge of heat rushing through her. It took several beats for her to register the fact that he was demanding to know her reasons for not including him.

"Why would you want to be involved in baby furniture, Luke? You said you didn't want children. I'm just trying to be sensitive to your feelings."

It was only half a lie. She was trying to be sensitive.

But her feelings for Luke were growing too big, too fast. And he had her dead to rights. She was doing her darnedest to keep him at arm's length. Even though he wasn't making it easy.

"It doesn't matter what I want or don't want," he said carefully. "There's just what is. This is my child, too. I'd appreciate it if you would consult me in the future. About everything."

"Okay. The disposable diaper aisle is pretty daunting. Some input on absorbency would be helpful. Not to mention wipes, in terms of scented or fragrance free," she said, starting to lift the long, awkwardly shaped box from the back of her SUV. The rear seat folded down, extending the trunk so it would accommodate the crib and mattress.

"What are you doing?" he asked sharply.

"I have to figure out how to get this inside."

"Stand back. This is man's work. Marchetti's my name, fetching and carrying's my game."

She was looking directly at him when he said that, and she studied him. He didn't look tense at all, not the way he had recently when mentioning his last name.

"What happened?" she asked. "I sense a thaw in the cold war."

"Really?"

He hefted the box from the car and rested it on his strong shoulder. It was such an inherently masculine movement that it made her mouth go dry.

"I know you, Luke," she said, a slightly breathless note in her voice. That was so true. Later she would wrestle with how, why and what a problem it was that she knew him so well. "Have you come to terms with your situation?"

He carried the crib into her condo and set it in her

empty third bedroom. He returned to the kitchen, not even out of breath or having worked up a sweat, she thought with mild annoyance as she handed him the cold can of soda she'd just taken from the refrigerator.

He took a long swig, then met her gaze. "I just told you my siblings came to see me today."

"I love being right," she said. "The twenty bucks is nice, too."

His only comment was a quick grin. Then he turned serious again. "They wanted to let me know that their feelings haven't changed. Rosie told me that Dad has kept his distance until I'm ready to talk."

She nodded. "Smart man." Studying his thoughtful expression, she added, "So what did you want to discuss with me that comes under the heading of billable hours?"

"My options with my biological father's business. The Marchettis are willing to give me all the time I need to make a decision, but it's not fair to them, or especially good for Marchetti's Incorporated, to drag this out."

Madison leaned back against the counter and folded her arms at her waist.

He looked at her. "As I see it I have three options—sell the accounting business, let someone else run it and remain as the majority stockholder and work for Marchetti's—" he hesitated a moment then said "—or take over the company that my biological father passed on to me."

"You don't need my advice," she said.

"But I'd like your opinion. What do you think I should do?"

"My money is on plan B. It's a win-win situation for you. It's a large, fiscally sound, profitable company. Income from that, along with your financial interest in Marchetti's would be nothing to sneeze at.''

"Not to mention keeping the business open so as not to contribute to the unemployment rate," he said dryly.

She nodded, then shrugged. "Call me a softie, but it's certainly something to take into consideration."

She studied him as he stood across from her and leaned back against the counter, crossing one ankle over the other. He set his soda can beside him and folded muscular arms over the masculine expanse of his chest. The blatantly male pose made her mouth go dry again and her heart go a gazillion miles a minute. Everything he did was so marvelously male. Why should it continue to surprise her? Or affect her, as in reaching out to her femininity?

"So are you going to keep me in suspense?" she asked, taking a deep breath to draw air into lungs suddenly empty of oxygen.

"I'm leaning toward plan C," he admitted.

"Leaving Marchetti's and running the accounting business," she clarified, to make sure they were discussing the same plan.

He nodded. "As you said, it's a large, lucrative company." A gleam stole into his eyes, as if he'd suddenly thought of a plan to end world hunger.

She shook her head. "What, Luke?"

"Handling the account would be quite a feather in your cap," he said. "Who takes care of legal matters for the accounting firm?"

She shrugged. "Jim Mallery said that your father had established legal counsel somewhere else. Jim drew up the will because of the sensitive nature of the situation with Flo and Tom and your father. Why?"

"Having the account would undoubtedly go a long way toward helping you reach your career goal."

Madison stared at him. "I can see the wheel spinning, but I'm not entirely certain that the hamster's still alive. What's going on in that brain of yours?"

"If I take over the accounting business, I can choose my own legal counsel."

"Even if you merely retain controlling interest, you could do that. But the real question is whether or not you would trust me with it." As much as his actions showed concern about her, she wouldn't delude herself into believing that that had been his primary motive. "Moving next door to watch over me is not the behavior of a man given to leaps of faith where I'm concerned."

He put his hands on his hips. "I know I've been acting a little over the top lately, Maddie. But a lot has happened," he said.

That was the biggest understatement she'd ever heard. "I'll grant you that. But this discussion still begs the question—why would you do anything to further my career?"

"To help you meet your personal goal of becoming a partner. I would insist that you handle *just* that account from home while you take care of the baby. And marry me."

Chapter Nine

Luke watched Maddie's eyes grow wide with surprise. He also computed the exact shade of green that told him she'd reached her maximum anger quotient, and her volcano was about to erupt.

She straightened and put her hands on her hips. "I cut you some slack about moving in next door. Don't ever make the mistake of believing that I don't have a backbone."

"Nothing could be farther from the truth."

"I'm willing to concede that I need to contact you about everything regarding the baby, including the furniture. Never again will I assume anything and make up your mind for you." She took a deep breath. "But you need to back off. Baby decisions are one thing, but this crosses the line."

"Joe told me to do it," he said.

"Your brother doesn't get a vote."

"I think it's a solution."

"For who? It seems to me that you're the one who benefits," she accused.

"How do you figure?"

"You're in control."

"How so?"

"Keep me at home. Throw me a crumb of legal work. I'll be under your thumb."

"Why do you assume that's my motive?"

"What else could it be? It's obvious you don't have deep feelings for me. If I wasn't carrying your baby, would you have asked me to marry you?"

Would he? He'd been convinced he would never have deep feelings for any woman and had almost been willing to settle. Then there was Maddie, and now she was pregnant. Everything had changed. He wasn't sure what he would have done. And he didn't think that was the issue. "The objection is overruled."

"Who made you the judge?" she demanded.

"I'm thinking about you and the baby. You've said you don't want hired help raising the child. How do you expect to go to the office every day unless you employ someone? Something tells me that Addison, Abernathy and Cooke won't be very sympathetic about an unhappy, outspoken infant sharing office space with you."

"You're using my words against me."

"I'm just being practical, Maddie. If you insist on remaining a single mother, you can't have it both ways. An unmarried mother carries all the responsibility."

"Some married mothers do that, too," she snapped.

"Not if they were married to me. I'm offering you the option of sharing the load."

"And what do you get out of it?"

The expectant look on her face made him feel like he was on a game show. Right answer and he won a million bucks. Wrong one and the buzzer blasted him into losing-contestant oblivion.

"I get to do the right thing," he finally said.

He could almost hear that buzzer when her shoulders slumped and the light went out of her eyes.

"Be still my heart," she said, fluttering a hand over her chest. "Words like that could turn a girl's head."

"I'm trying to be honest with you. What do you want from me?"

"Nothing." She glared at him. "I have assured you that I will never deny you your child. In time you'll see that I'm telling the truth. In the meantime, the fact that we share this baby doesn't give you the right to steamroll me."

"That's not what this is about."

"If you truly believe that, then you're CFO of fantasyland. Face it, Luke. You moved in next door to *watch* me, not watch over me. Then you have the nerve to accuse me of trying to keep you at a distance. If I am, do you blame me?"

"I'm just trying to do the right thing," he said again.

"And taking it to the next level," she said. "The truth is that I'm paying the price because your parents lied to you. I was just trying to do the right thing, but you refuse to give me the benefit of the doubt. Your parents acted out of love, and you won't even speak to them."

Her accusation hit a little too close to the mark. It pricked his conscience, now that he'd had time to assimilate what had happened. "Have you ever been lied to?" he asked defensively.

"Probably. But I can't give you specifics because I don't keep a running tally."

This wasn't about him or her. It was about their unborn child. "I mean lied to in the most basic and elemental way possible."

"No." She looked at the ceiling for a moment, then back at him. "But everyone has issues, Luke. Including me. I was an unwanted accident. I know firsthand what it feels like to be discarded."

"Then you should appreciate what I'm trying to do."

"I would if I thought you could ever—"

"What?"

"Forget it." She shook her head. "No one is perfect, which makes raising perfect children an impossible task. That scares me to death," she said, putting her hands over her abdomen in an unconsciously protective gesture. "But I resent the fact that you're trying to use that fear against me to get your way and then stoop to calling it helping."

"I was just trying to give you the opportunity to stay at home with our child and still keep a hand in your career. I was trying to give you the best of all possible worlds."

"That's what it looks like on the surface. An offer like that should earn you wings and a halo from feminists everywhere. But I know it isn't about me and the baby. It's about you."

How could it be about him? She was the mother of his child. He had to take care of them both. What else did she want from him? "You're wrong, Maddie."

"Then we need to agree to disagree." She sighed. "Normally I would like nothing better than a good philosophical argument. After all, that's what I do for a living. But I'm tired, Luke. Please leave."

Anger surged through him. He wanted to convince her that he had her best interests at heart. But when he saw the weary look in her eyes, the dark circles beneath, his anger drained away. The same heart that wanted her best interests went out to her. He wanted to pull her against him and hold her. No woman had ever stirred his blood like Maddie. And the way she'd gone on the attack...

He'd come close to telling her she was breathtaking— so beautiful when she was angry. But somehow he knew if he'd said that, instead of just asking him to leave, she'd be physically bouncing him out the door. He made a mental note to never underestimate the adrenaline pump of a pregnant redhead. But he had bigger problems than that. Like how to convince her to let him take care of her.

But he knew she was right about having her own issues. He sensed that she wanted something more from him. And he wasn't certain what it was or if he was capable of it.

"All right, Maddie." He walked to the front door with her right behind him. He opened it and looked down at her. "If you need anything—"

"I won't," she said, flipping the switch to turn on the porch light.

"How can you be so sure?"

"Because I never had anyone to turn to. I learned to be self-sufficient." She sighed as she leaned against the open door. Tears glistened in her eyes but didn't fall. "I'm not sure what's worse. Being an accident with no right to a life. Or having someone around who thinks he can run that life better than me."

"Maddie, I—"

"There's nothing more to say, Luke. Good night."

She closed the door, and a great black emptiness gaped inside him.

He put his palm against the solid oak barrier wondering why her words had sounded so much like goodbye.

And the look in her eyes showed him that an unscalable wall had gone up. But most important, why did he care so very much about the distance she'd put between them?

Madison carried her overnight bag up the wooden cabin stairs. Taking in a big breath of San Bernardino Mountain air, she decided Rosie was right. This was a wonderful getaway place. She'd thought Luke's sister a tad pushy when she wouldn't accept excuses and had urged her to use it for the weekend. Now she made a mental note to send her flowers as a thank-you.

When she reached the wooden deck leading to the door, she fished the key Rosie had given her from her purse and let herself inside. She set her bag down just inside the door and opened the horizontal blinds. A large, circular fire pit dominated the center of the living room. Against one long wall rested a sofa and at a right angle, the matching plaid love seat in shades of beige, hunter green and maroon. Color-coordinated wingback chairs sat across from them, and occasional oak tables comfortably placed at the corners completed the grouping.

Exploring upstairs, she found several bedrooms and a loft with pool table and dart board. The master bedroom was on the first floor, and she put her suitcase on the battered and scarred cedar chest at the foot of the king-size bed.

Staring at it she said, "It looks as if it's been through five children." Glancing around, she said, "I don't know what to do first—take a walk or start that bestseller I haven't had time for." She thought for a moment and said aloud, "Walk. Not smart to come all this way and cocoon inside."

After changing into white shorts that used to be loose but were now hugging her a bit too tightly, a lime-green T-shirt and matching socks, followed by sneakers, she left the cabin to be one with Mother Nature.

Several hours later Madison returned, pleasantly tired, with soul refilled, replenished and shored up after gulping fresh air, the sweet fragrance of pine and looking her fill at a clear, blue, smog-free California sky. When she opened the cabin door, she realized Mother Nature in person couldn't have prepared her for the sight of the man standing there.

"Luke!"

His feet were spread wide apart and his arms folded over his broad, impressive chest. He could be the conquering hero from any time period in history—arrogant, confident and ready for his reward. And he'd never looked better.

God help her, she wanted to throw herself in his arms.

"What are you doing here?" she asked. "Are you following me? Because if you are—"

He held his hands up. "Before you blow your stack, let me ask you something. Did my sister by any chance suggest that you come up here for the weekend?"

"*Suggest* is a wimpy word for what your sister did," she answered. "She all but offered to carry me here on her back."

He nodded as if that revelation didn't come as a big surprise. "I'm sorry, Maddie. I had nothing to do with this, except for mentioning to Rosie that you refused to see me and weren't taking my phone calls. She talked me into coming here, too. Some song and dance about forgetting to shut the water off. It's standard operating procedure since the flood."

"Flood?"

He nodded. "Fran came up to use the cabin, and a pipe under the kitchen sink had somehow broken. Water was everywhere. Either Rosie or my mother or both were responsible for sending Alex up to bail her out."

"And look what happened to them," she said, remembering the recently married couple. Instead of anger, even she heard the faintly wistful note in her voice.

"Yeah," he said. And there was no mistaking the marriage-is-a-fate-worse-than-death note in his voice. "My mother and sister attribute some sort of mystical, matchmaking power to this cabin. They're convinced that couples who come up here alone together are doomed to fall in love."

"'Doomed'?" she said, arching an eyebrow. "Interesting choice of words."

But that didn't come as a surprise to her. Nothing he had said would lead her to believe he cared about her that way. And as soon as she could manage it, she would shake off her disappointment.

"I didn't mean it like that," he countered. "All I'm trying to say is we were set up."

"Looks that way," she agreed.

He ran a hand through his hair. "It will be dark soon. How do you feel about sleeping under the same roof tonight? Separate bedrooms, of course."

The expression on his face changed to hungry and intense when he mentioned sleeping arrangements. And there was a corresponding yearning in the core of her femininity at the very male way he looked at her.

Why did she respond so strongly to him? And how did she feel about that? Madison watched him take in her bare legs, slightly rounded tummy and T-shirt-embraced breasts. The spark of appreciation in his eyes made her as breathless as her high-altitude walk. It also made her heart race, her skin tingle and her legs tremble. Not to mention her feeling of fear. She'd worried about the flimsy Sheetrock wall separating their condos being enough. How could she possibly spend the night under the same roof with Luke Marchetti and find the will to resist him?

"I'll leave," she offered. "After all, it's your family's place."

She expected him to deny that they were family when he shook his head. "No. If anyone leaves it will be me. I need to wring my sister's neck, anyway."

That reminded her what he'd said about his mother and the cabin's magic matchmaking properties. She had the twenty bucks to prove he'd had a conversation with his siblings. But he hadn't said anything about where he stood with his mom and dad. "Have you spoken to your parents since—"

He shook his head. "And before you start in on me, I could ask you the same thing. Have you told your folks about the baby?"

He would have made a good attorney, she decided. If you find yourself in a corner, go on the attack. She'd thought about breaking the news to her parents, but the very idea made her want to throw up. "No. But my situation is completely different. Your parents have always supported you. I don't even speak to mine on a regular basis."

"Coward."

She started to deny it but couldn't. Shrugging, she said, "*Coward* is such a strong word."

"Don't you think they deserve to know they're going to be grandparents?"

"Based on the loving way I was raised?" she asked sarcastically. "No."

He folded his arms over his chest. "Sooner or later you've got to tell them. They're going to wonder about the baby crying in the background when you talk on the phone."

"No. They don't wonder about me at all." She studied his narrow-eyed gaze and knew what he was thinking. "This is completely different from choosing the best time to break the news to you."

"If you say so."

"Look, Luke. You're not walking in my shoes any more than I am in yours. My relationship with my parents is completely different from what you have with yours. We go months without speaking. You hardly went a day, at least before all this happened. Call them."

"I'll make you a deal. You call yours, then I'll call mine."

Why did he care if she notified her folks? What was in it for him? Scratch that. She was turning into the world's biggest cynic. Currently, Luke held the world title to that honor.

But what did she have to lose by agreeing? Maybe she could get him to blink first in this stalemate with his mom and dad. "Okay. When I get home I'll see if I can get in touch with them."

"What about now?"

She should have known he would call her bluff. "I don't want to rack up long-distance charges."

"I think we can absorb the cost. Besides, if you're right, it will be a short call. Quit stalling, Maddie." He held out the receiver. "No guts, no glory."

He thought she was gutless? She took the phone. "I'm only doing this for you. It's the only reason. I'm sacrificing myself so that you'll talk to your folks. Diplomacy. That's what this is."

"Whatever you say, slick."

She straightened her spine, squared her shoulders, then turned away from him as she punched in the east coast area code followed by her parents' number. Let them be out of the country, she prayed. They'd never been around for the milestones in her life, why would they be there now?

It rang a scant three times before a familiar, cultured female voice answered, "Hello?"

"Mother? It's Maddie—Madison."

"Hello, dear. What a lovely surprise. How are you?" Claudia Wainright actually sounded pleased to hear from her.

Shocked, she managed to say, "I'm fine, really good, Mother." If only the butterflies in her stomach would take a five-minute break so that her voice would lose the too-animated, yet nervous note. "How are you and Father?"

"Very well, dear. What a coincidence that you phoned. Just this morning Winston and I were saying that it's been too long since we've seen you. We're talking about coming to California for a visit."

"You are?" So she'd lied a few moments ago when she'd said they didn't wonder about her.

"He can't get away just yet. What about Thanksgiving?"

Panic threatened. She would be approaching her sixth month with no way to hide her condition. Then it struck her. Was Luke right about her? Was she the type to withhold information and call it sensitivity? No way. It was time to show her mettle and prove him wrong.

"I'd like very much to see you both. But first I have some wonderful news, Mother. Are you sitting down?"

"Yes." There was a question in her voice. "What is

it, dear? You haven't gone L.A. and had your fanny tattooed?''

"Mother! Of course I don't have a tattoo." She glanced over her shoulder and saw Luke grin. She turned away before she got caught up in the way the dimples bracketing his mouth made her want to kiss him.

There was a laugh on the other end of the line. "Sorry, dear, I couldn't resist. Now, tell me your news."

She let out a long breath. "I'm going to have a baby," she said, then held her breath and braced herself for the blast of cold air.

On the other end of the line there was a pause that could only be called pregnant. "I'm going to be a grandmother?"

"That's right," she said firmly. "I'm very happy about it," she added, in case there was any question. She figured her mother would be happier about the tattoo.

"Congratulations, dear. May I ask who the father is?" Instead of the expected coolness, her tone held nothing but curiosity.

Madison sat down in the chair beside the phone table. "Luke Marchetti."

"Of the Italian restaurant Marchettis?"

"That's the one. You've heard of him?"

"Only the family's reputation."

"Good or bad?" Madison had to know.

"Very good. But I don't believe I've received a wedding invitation."

"That's because I'm not planning a wedding."

"He has asked you to marry him?"

"Yes."

"I see."

Madison couldn't tell what she saw, and the meager

amount of courage she'd managed to muster disappeared. "Look, Mother, I'm not at home. Can I call you in a day or two when we can chat longer about this?"

"I'll look forward to it, dear. Do I have your permission to share this news with your father?"

"Do you have to?"

"Not if you'd rather I didn't. But don't you think he deserves to know?"

Didn't I deserve a childhood? she wanted to retort. But that was immature, and she was a grown woman, on the brink of motherhood. It was time to act like it.

"Of course."

"Good."

Relief flooded Madison. The news was out, and the world hadn't ended. In fact, her mother actually sounded eager to talk again. Spontaneously she blurted out, "I love you, Mother."

"I love you, too, dear. Goodbye."

Stunned, Madison just looked at the phone. She couldn't remember the last time, if ever, her mother had said those words to her. She didn't know what to make of it. Some people called babies "little miracles." Is that what had just happened? When she continued to stare at the phone in her hand, Luke took it from her and rested it on the cradle.

"She took it badly?" he asked.

Without the phone to hold, Madison twisted her fingers together. "I'd have to say no."

"So she's upset that I'm the father?"

Madison shook her head. "Your reputation has advanced clear to the east coast. She's heard good things about the restaurant Marchettis." She met his gaze. "And don't tell me you aren't one."

"The thought never entered my mind. But you look

shell-shocked. Is she put out that you're not getting married?''

''We've primarily had a phone relationship over the years, so I've perfected the technique of translating every nuance of every tone in her voice. And I don't think she was annoyed.''

''So what did she hit the roof about?''

She looked at him and shrugged helplessly. ''Nothing.''

''Then it's safe to say it went well?''

She nodded. ''Yes.''

''Then why do you look as if your world just shook like an 8.2 on the Richter scale?''

She wasn't sure. But her earliest memories included her coming to terms with her parents nonchalance. She knew how painful it was without love. This thawing of her mother *did* shake her up. She was confused, but relieved and happy. Actually looking forward to speaking with her mother again to see if it had been a temporary aberration. But the experience had been good. And if not for Luke, she would never have called.

She moved beside him, stood on tiptoe and kissed his lean cheek. His hands came loosely around her waist, but she quickly backed away because she couldn't trust herself.

''Thank you for shaming me into calling,'' she said. ''You're very often exasperating, but sometimes very wise.''

Her heart dropped when he grinned. ''You're welcome. I have another brilliant idea.''

''And humble, too.''

''Let me take you to dinner to celebrate.''

Madison felt as if the weight of the world had lifted

from her shoulders. A celebration sounded like a wonderful idea. "You're on, Luke."

Several hours later they stood on the deck of the cabin, staring up at the stars. Luke looked down at Maddie and thought there wasn't a celestial body in the sky more beautiful or sexy or curvy than her. He'd noticed that her previously flat stomach was slightly rounded now. She grew more beautiful every day, and he had a feeling when she was nine months pregnant, she would take his breath away. And he admired her—her spirit and courage. She was determined to take care of herself and the baby without help. Why couldn't she believe that she would never have to do it alone?

She shivered and rubbed her arms.

"Are you cold?" he asked.

"I didn't realize the mountains cooled off so much at night."

He took his windbreaker from the wooden railing beside him and dragged it around her shoulders. When he pulled it across her chest, he couldn't seem to let go. He gazed into her eyes, and it took every last drop of his willpower to keep from kissing her.

"That was a wonderful restaurant," she said, a breathless, husky quality to her voice. "Who would have guessed such a charming place would be tucked away up here in the mountains."

Reluctantly he stuck his hands in his pockets. "Casual Elegance is one of my family's favorites."

He was getting used to saying "my family" again. After the visit from his siblings, he didn't feel as though the DNA police were going to jump out of the bushes when he said it and arrest him for being a fraud. And Maddie had supported him from the beginning. He was grateful to her for being his anchor in a turbulent time. She had been there for him, and he vowed to do the same for her.

He had really enjoyed watching her by candlelight in the intimate, forty-five-seat restaurant. The lovely, sexy way her curls had framed her face, turning golden when they caught the light, was branded in his memory forever. If he lived to be a hundred, he would never forget the sweet, seductive picture she'd made or how much he'd wanted her. Wanted her still, he amended.

He had never wanted a woman this badly. She was always on his mind. Why? What was it about her that grabbed him and held on, never letting go?

"That was the best pesto linguine I've ever had," she continued. "Not that Marchettis restaurants don't make a fine pesto," she quickly added.

"It's not our specialty," he said.

He and Maddie had perfected a specialty of their own—going up in flames without warning. It seemed like forever since he'd tasted her lips, felt the exquisite softness of her breasts pressed against his chest, held her fragile body protectively against his own. She was femininity personified, a contrast to the hard angles and strong planes of his male body.

He put his hands on her shoulders and then slid them down, curving his palms around her upper arms. "Maddie, I—"

"You're good, Marchetti," she said, a little breathlessly.

In the light of the full moon, he could see her eyes grow wider. Did she know how very badly he wanted to kiss her? Did she know that he intended to do just that? Was she trying to distract him? He could see the pulse at the base of her throat beating wildly and suspected that she needed to be kissed as much as he needed to do the kissing. But he would play along with her distraction—just a little. Just long enough to heighten all of her senses.

"Okay," he agreed. "Care to enlighten me? How am I good?"

"You really sidetracked me today. Not only did we *not* decide which one of us was leaving the cabin, I called my parents, but you did not call yours."

He grinned. He'd wondered if she would figure that out. "You're right. I am good."

"So are you leaving? Or should I?"

"Neither." He rested his hands on her shoulders, moving his right thumb up so that he could caress the underside of her slender jaw. Her shiver at his touch filled him with male satisfaction. "That winding mountain road is dangerous at night. We're adults. We can be trusted alone together."

"All evidence to the contrary," she said, pressing her hands over her abdomen.

"Curves can be dangerous," he admitted. And he wasn't talking about the road. "But if it will make you happy, I'll go."

She sighed. "No. You're right. I couldn't live with myself if something happened to you."

"So you do care about me," he said, carefully putting a teasing note in his voice to camouflage how very much her answer meant.

"Of course. You're the father of my child. We're friends—"

"Friends? I'm disappointed in you. You're a lawyer. Words are your life. And that's the best you can come up with to describe us? Sometimes actions speak louder—and more eloquently—than words."

He tunneled his fingers into her thick curls and let his thumb explore her full, trembling mouth. Just for a moment. When he couldn't wait any longer, he bent his head and touched his lips to hers. Her small female moan of pleasure was like fuel to the sparks he'd created. Passion exploded into flame. Sliding his arm around her waist, he pulled her full against him. Her mouth, stiff at first, softened and yielded to him with only the slightest coaxing. She was incredibly delicate, so womanly, warm and willing that she stole the breath from his lungs.

Without hesitation her hands moved up his chest to encircle his neck. He and Maddie were pressed together from chest to thigh, yet it wasn't close enough. Luke lightly ran his tongue over the soft seam of her lips until she opened to him. He stroked the sweet interior, not satisfied until he felt her tremble with need and her shallow breathing matched his own. She felt small, fragile, vulnerable in his arms. This wisp of a woman brought out his protective instincts like no other. He wanted to keep her safe. He *wanted* her. Only her.

"Maddie," he whispered into her ear. "If we don't stop, I think I'm going to carry you inside and have my way with you."

She pulled back and looked at him, eyes huge and beautiful. "Luke, we can't."

"Why?"

"We've been over it before. Please don't make this difficult."

"It wouldn't be—if you'd marry me."

"If only I—"

From *if only* it was a hop, skip and a jump to *yes*. "So when are we going to set the date?" he asked.

Chapter Ten

Stunned, Madison backed away and stared up at him. She missed his warmth as the cool mountain air whistled past the cabin walls and caressed her hot cheeks. And *hot* was definitely the operative word—inside and out.

One kiss. One touch of his mouth to hers and she'd been putty in his hands again. And she knew he knew it. Because this time he was using her feelings for him to get what he wanted. It felt so wonderful to be wanted—*desired*. Loved? That was going too far. But somehow he sensed the depth of her emotions, because he'd gone in for the kill at her most vulnerable moment.

She took a deep breath. "You know, this just has to be said. You've got all the sensitivity of a charging rhino. How stupid do you think I am?"

"You're one of the brightest people I've ever met—male or female. Why?"

"Because I can't help wondering why in the world you would think I'd fall for this manipulation?"

"What are you talking about?"

"Get my motor running, then pop the question in a moment of—"

"Passion?" he asked, one dark eyebrow rising.

"Weakness," she clarified.

"First of all, I resent the insinuation that I would be that underhanded." He ran his fingers through his hair. Was his hand shaking? "Second, I freely admit that women are beyond my sphere of expertise. But if your parents have no objection to a marriage, why do you? Why shouldn't we set the date?"

"One good reason is your assumption that just because they think it's okay I do."

"Those are the two words I want to hear."

She shook her head. "You're trying to steamroll me again."

"I know better than to try that with you, Maddie. It just seemed like a good idea to bring up the subject. Tell me that kiss didn't turn you on, too, and we'll drop this whole thing."

"It didn't turn me on," she said, raising her gaze as far as his shirt collar. Maybe he wouldn't notice that she didn't quite look him in the eyes. Maybe he wouldn't guess that she was lying.

"You're lying," he charged. "I suppose it was someone else who moaned that sexy little moan just a few minutes ago."

"I never," she fibbed again.

"Yeah, you did. And you're breathing like you just finished a 10 K run."

She took a deep breath and slowly released it. "This is just another method of control," she accused. "You're trying to run the show."

"Do you blame me? You've been avoiding me for days."

"And for good reason, obviously."

"It's not obvious to me," he returned.

"We've already gone through this, Luke. This is all about you and what you want."

"Tell me again, Maddie. I didn't get it then. Maybe you can make me understand now."

"You're angry with your parents for not being honest with you. This obsession to marry me is nothing more than the manifestation of your need to keep the upper hand. You're determined to have control over this child. To do that you need to control the child's mother. Which is the only reason that you're so determined to marry me. And you'll use my mother and my r-reaction to your kiss against me. To get what you want."

"That's pretty harsh," he said, eyes narrowed dangerously.

"Really? As I see it, if you're not in control, you cut people out of your life, people who love you."

Like me.

The thought popped into her mind so unexpectedly she swayed slightly. If the railing hadn't been behind her to steady her, the jolt would have knocked her flat. He hadn't technically cut her out of his life, but only because she was the mother of his child. But he'd done everything except hire a private detective for surveillance to show that he didn't trust her. That created emotional distance, which was the same as cutting her out of his life.

Did she love him? Lord, she hoped not. But she had an awful feeling that all he had to do was say he loved her and she would follow him anywhere. And if he didn't feel it, enough to say it on his own, then she didn't want to hear it. She would never believe it.

He stared at her. "All I want is for this child to never

wonder about who his father is. The way I've had to wonder. I have questions that will never be answered.''

"Your parents could help you with some of them if you'd give them a chance."

"Yeah. But they robbed me of the chance to meet the man."

"Get over it, Luke. No one goes through life without missing opportunities. Some we blow ourselves. Some are taken out of our hands. But if you walk away from a beautiful relationship with your family, I guarantee the day will come when you'll kick yourself from here to kingdom come. You had the best possible male role model in Tom Marchetti. If you're a good father to this child, you have him to thank. And so do I. But look how you repaid him. You turned your back on your mother and him.''

"What does that have to do with marrying me?"

"I can't help wondering if running away is your pro-grammed response to disappointment. No one is perfect, Luke. If I don't do what you want, or this child ever lets you down, are you going to turn away? Take back your love? Like you have from your parents? Because they aren't perfect?"

Or never give love in the first place? Like you have with me? she wondered.

"That's not fair, Maddie. You can't compare what I've gone through with the ups and downs of parenting."

"You're the one who keeps throwing the probability of patterns up to me. Look at your own behavior. Why shouldn't I believe you would cut us out of your life if things don't go your way?"

"Are you trying to tell me that you're going to keep my child from me?"

She shook her head. "Nothing could be farther from

the truth. I'm just trying to make you see why I can't marry you. I know what it's like when you're not wanted. All my life I've struggled to win my parents' love.''

"That's not what I saw earlier. Seems like you and your mom got along fine."

She shrugged. "I haven't figured out what was up with her. Maybe it's always been there and she didn't know how to show it. Or maybe she's been abducted by aliens and a beta unit left in her place."

"What's your point?" he asked, fisting his hands on his hips.

"Your parents showed you their love every chance they got. And the first time it's tested, you take yours back."

"Even if you're right, what's that got to do with you and me and our baby?"

"Whether or not my folks loved me is irrelevant, because I perceived that they didn't. I know how much it hurts when you're not loved. There's no way I will sentence this baby to life with a parent who doesn't love him."

Or his mother, she added silently.

"Maddie, be reasonable."

She folded her arms over her chest, trying to control the shivering. It wasn't the mountain air making her tremble. The cold she felt came clear from her soul. "I think I'm being eminently fair, logical, rational and prudent. There's nothing more to say. Good night, Luke. I'll be leaving first thing in the morning."

"Maddie, listen—"

She went to the door, then glanced back at him. "I have listened, and there's nothing you've said that changes my mind. I have a doctor's appointment on

Monday—1:00 p.m. You're welcome to be there. If you want.''

She went to the master bedroom and closed and locked the door. Then she lay on the bed and buried her face in the pillow so he wouldn't hear her cry.

All her life she'd been successful at everything she'd tried—except love. Being a failure at that hurt so much. She'd known it would. And it wasn't as if she hadn't tried to keep herself from falling for Luke. But she knew, the way a woman knows these things, that he was the only man for her. Why did he have to be a man who couldn't love her back?

They shared a child, a special little someone who would connect them for the rest of their lives. Somehow she had to find a way to keep him from knowing how very much it hurt that he couldn't care.

''So what brings you here, Son?'' Tom Marchetti had just opened the front door and stood there, looking as if everything was normal.

The only clue about the rift between them was that he hadn't automatically stepped back, assuming Luke would come inside. He was six foot two, taller than Luke. His once-dark hair was now liberally laced with gray, but his brown eyes still gleamed with his trademark intelligence.

Luke shifted from one foot to the other. ''At the cabin, over the weekend, Maddie and I—''

''You two went to the mountains?''

''Rosie set us up.''

''Ah'' was the only response from the older man.

''Anyway, I made a deal with Maddie. We both agreed to call our folks.'' He shrugged. ''She followed through and I didn't. So here I am.''

"It's good to see you, Son." Tom opened the door wider. "Come on into the kitchen. Your mother is busy, but you look like you could use a decent meal."

"That's Ma's line."

"So it is. I learned from the best."

They walked into the kitchen where more than once Luke had talked over a problem or two or ten with this man. Never knowing that they weren't connected by blood.

Luke pulled out one of the ladderback oak chairs, but he was too keyed-up to sit. It was time to get this all out in the open. "So you think Ma is the best? Even after what she did to you?"

"And what is it you think she did to me?"

"You took her back after she betrayed you with another man. My father," he added.

"I'm a selfish man, Luke." Tom cut a piece of chocolate cake and poured a glass of milk and set both in front of him.

"Selfish?" That didn't compute with the man he knew. "What do you mean?"

"I won't lie to you. I was angry about what your mother did. I left." He stood on the other side of the table and met his gaze. "I even tried to stop loving Flo."

"What happened?"

"The love wouldn't stop. And that's where the selfish part comes in. I wanted her in my life any way I could get her."

"That makes you weak, not selfish," he said.

Tom thought that over for a few moments. Then he nodded. "You're probably right. Without Flo I felt like a part of myself was missing. The light went out of my life. Everything I'd worked so hard for, and jeopardized my marriage for, didn't mean anything without her. If that makes me weak, then I'm guilty as charged.''

"So that's why you took her back after she betrayed you?"

"She made a mistake. But so did I. I forgot that relationships take work. It takes two to make or break a marriage. I assume half the blame as well as half the rewards. I didn't just take her back, I begged her not to leave me.''

Stunned, Luke sat down, leaving the cake and milk still untouched. "Did you know she was carrying another man's child at the time?"

He nodded. "She was up-front and honest. At first she refused to reconcile because of it. And I could have let that come between us. But it would have meant giving up your mother. That was something I couldn't do." He looked down at his clasped hands for a moment. "The choices we make shape our lives. I *chose* to be a father to you. There are decisions I've made that I do regret, but not that one. I love you. And I won't qualify it by saying as if you were my own son. You *are* my son.''

Luke was humbled by the sincerity he saw in his father's face. Would he ever have Tom Marchetti's strength? Was it enough to grow up under his steady, guiding hand?

Tom walked over to the kitchen cupboards, opening each until he found what he wanted. He reached up and took out the mended crystal bowl that was always on the Thanksgiving dinner table.

He brought it over to Luke and handed it to him. "The five of you have always wondered about this. To Flo and me it's a symbol of what we almost lost. I broke it when I found out about you. I left the same day. She saved the pieces because it was my mother's. When I came to my senses, Flo and I patched it up and put it back together. We did the same to our life. When we need a reminder, out comes the bowl.''

Before Maddie, Luke wouldn't have understood feelings that strong. He did now. Because of Maddie. Was it love? He'd doubted for so long that it would happen to him, he wasn't sure he would recognize it if it waltzed up and kissed him full on the mouth. He envied the depth of feeling that had brought Flo and Tom Marchetti through trial by fire. Their love had withstood the test and come out stronger.

But he still couldn't reconcile why they had kept him in the dark about his biological father. If Brad Stephenson hadn't left a will, Luke wouldn't know about him even now. There had been clues, but he'd had no reason to doubt his parentage. Did he wish to go back? To have never known? But he did know, and he had questions.

''Why didn't you and Mom tell me?'' he said, tapping his chest. ''Didn't it occur to you that I might want to know?''

''We discussed the situation—your father, Flo and me. Sometimes saying nothing is the best course of action.''

''It's a lie of omission.''

''Technically, yes. But it seemed best to raise you in a large, loving family. Kids want to fit in. A situation like that would have set you apart, caused problems that were unnecessary. Did I treat you any differently from your brothers or sister? Did you suspect that you were special?''

Luke smiled at the word. ''I never guessed.''

Tom nodded with satisfaction. ''Then I'm damn proud of the job I did,'' he said.

Luke suddenly got it. The fact that he'd never guessed the secret was a testament to Tom Marchetti's strength and decency. And a profound measure of his love.

He got up, rounded the table and hugged his father. "You're the best man I've ever met."

"I wish you'd had a chance to meet Brad. He was a good man."

"You're not angry with him?" Luke asked, amazed.

Again he tried to imagine what it would feel like. He hadn't raised a child yet, but his feelings of protectiveness grew stronger every day. If anyone shook up his child's life the way his own had been, he would want satisfaction.

Tom shrugged. "I was at first. But I can't blame him for facing his mortality and not wanting to leave this earth without you knowing about him. The fact that he didn't say anything all these years shows how much he loved you."

Luke nodded. "I guess I'm lucky."

"I guess you are," said a female voice.

He looked past his father and saw his mother standing in the doorway. "Hi, Ma," he said. "You're finished being busy."

She nodded. "You and your father have had enough time to talk."

Luke opened his arms and didn't miss the glitter of tears in her eyes just before she stepped into them.

"I've missed you," she said.

"Yeah. I've missed you guys, too." He looked at his father. "You're a very wise old man."

There was a suspicious brightness in his father's eyes, too, but he grinned. "I'm not comfortable with the 'very old' part, but the rest is true enough."

Luke laughed, then squeezed his mother's shoulder as

he looked at Tom. "I'm sorry I've been such a jerk. Maddie says I'm exasperating."

Flo smiled. "She's good for you. I'm glad you had her support through all of this. But as tough as it's been, I still think we did the right thing. If I had to make the decision again, I would do it the same way."

Luke grinned at her. "It's a good thing I didn't find out when I was a teenager. Most of them rebel for no apparent reason. I had one and didn't know it."

Flo smiled. "I can't help wishing you'd never had to go through the pain. But at least you were a grown man when you found out. As an adult, you were able to assimilate the information faster and speed up the maturity process."

Tom kissed her cheek. "In spite of teenagers' temporary insanity, children learn what they live. If they grow up with security and love, it becomes the cornerstone of their life."

Luke thought about Maddie, growing up believing she was an unwanted accident. She'd had no cornerstone to trust that anyone would love her. And she'd not given herself to any man—until him. What did that mean? She'd said her virginity was a burden she'd wanted gone, but he didn't buy it. And how did he feel about her? She was carrying his child.

He walked over to the island, then turned back to them, folding his arms over his chest. "I hope I can be as good a parent to my child as you guys have been to me."

"A child needs two parents. You and Maddie have to work together and present a united front," his mother said.

"What are you trying to say, Ma?"

"Everyone accuses me of matchmaking. I refuse to

be any clearer than that," she said, clamping her lips tightly together.

Tom laughed. "You're as subtle as an earthquake, Florence Marchetti."

Luke shook his head. "I've asked Maddie to marry me three times. And she turned me down flat."

"Then I guess we can't say third time's the charm," Flo commented. "Don't give up, sweetheart. I'd bet Grandma Marchetti's silver salt and pepper shakers that Maddie cares about you very much. I've always said you two were meant for each other."

"Yes, you have," Luke agreed.

But he couldn't imagine what she saw that he didn't. He just knew that somehow he had to smooth the rift with Maddie. He remembered the last look he'd seen on her face, the profound hurt. Could he put the smile back on her face, the twinkle in her eyes?

He looked at his folks, both grinning broadly at him. It had taken one miracle to fix things with them. Could he hope for another with Maddie?

Chapter Eleven

Luke decided to test the formula for his Maddie miracle by first mending fences with big brother Nick. He knew Maddie had a doctor's appointment today, and he planned to be there. But before he could face her again, he wanted to get the rest of his life back on track. Which was why he was at the corporate offices of Marchetti's Incorporated without an appointment, staring at Nick's secretary and waiting for her to blink first.

"Mr. Marchetti said he didn't want to be disturbed," she told him again.

"I'm his brother," he reminded her. And I've just gone through a personal crisis of monumental proportions so let me in, he added silently.

"I recognized you right away, Mr. Marchetti," she said. "But orders are orders. You don't have an appointment. He wasn't expecting you. And he didn't distinguish between family or anyone else. His precise words were 'If you value your job, no one gets through that door.' Period."

Family. The word inspired a sense of satisfaction, in spite of his annoyance at the woman. He *was* part of the family. His place had always been secure. It had just taken him time to see that.

"I have to be somewhere, but I need to see my brother first. I won't take up much of his time. If he's too busy to see me, he's going to have to tell me himself," Luke said, charging past her desk. "I promise your job is safe."

He knocked once on his brother's office door, then went inside. Nick was leaning back in his chair with the phone to his ear. "You're pregnant, Ab. Managing the restaurant is tiring. If you get tired, sit. Being married to the boss has its privileges, even though you don't want any special favors because of it. That's what I love about you."

He saw Luke in the doorway and grinned broadly. When his secretary appeared, he waved her away and indicated that Luke should take a seat.

Luke took the high road and didn't give the woman his I-told-you-so look. He smiled politely and closed the door. Then he sat on the corner of his brother's desk and rested his linked hands on a jeans-clad thigh. He admired his brother for keeping sacred this time with his wife, even if it was just a phone call. "Tell Abby I said hi."

"Luke says hi, honey." He listened for a moment, then laughed. "Yeah, I'll tell him. I love you," he said with a tender note he saved for his wife. Then he rested the phone on the cradle.

"Your secretary is a pit bull," Luke said.

"Yeah. It's her best quality." He leaned back in his chair and rested linked hands over his abdomen. "What can I do for you?"

"Listen to me grovel."

He grinned. "There's nothing I'd like better." He thought for a moment and amended the statement. "Actually that's not entirely true. There are other things I like better, but they involve my wife."

Luke envied his brother. A woman he loved, who loved him back, and a baby on the way. Nick had it all. "What did Abby tell you to tell me?"

"That it's about time you snapped out of it and quit being a jerk to me."

"Don't be so paranoid. I was a jerk to everyone."

"Seriously, Luke, it's good to see you. I've missed you."

"Yeah. Me, too." He stood and folded his arms over his chest. "I had a talk with Mom and Dad."

Nick raised an eyebrow. "Really?"

Luke grinned at his feigned surprise. "Nice try. But don't ever leave your day job for the stage. You already know."

"Okay. Mom called. She and Dad were very happy."

"Look, Nick, I'm sorry I've been such an ass. But I'm okay now."

"No, you're probably still an ass," his brother commented with a twinkle in his brown eyes. "But at least you've come to terms with everything and again assumed your rightful place in the family."

Luke let one corner of his mouth curve up. "I'm going to pretend that my apology has been accepted."

"I just want to know when you're planning to come back to work."

"The guy who's been running the accounting business is doing a great job. I plan to put him in charge permanently. If it ain't broke, don't fix it. So I guess now can't be too soon for me," Luke answered fervently.

"You're not exactly dressed for it. Jeans and T-shirt is pushing the limit for casual Friday, and it's Monday."

Luke ran a hand through his hair. "I have to meet Maddie at the obstetrician."

"Everything okay with the baby?" Nick asked. "Little Nick is looking forward to playing with his cousin when she comes out."

"So you're having a boy and I'm having a girl? What to expect when you're expecting according to Nick Marchetti?"

"Right on, Bro." He studied Luke. "Seriously, what's going on with you?"

"At last report the baby was fine. Everything is progressing normally. Everything, that is, except for the baby's parents."

"Would you like to elaborate?"

"I've asked Maddie to marry me three times, and she's turned me down. She's agreed to share custody, but is adamant that she won't tie herself to a man who doesn't love her."

"Do you? Love her, I mean."

Luke rubbed the back of his neck. "She was a virgin, Nick."

His brother whistled. "Now there's a statement. But it doesn't answer my question. Do you love her?"

"I care about her." He shook his head. "I've been with a lot of women. In fact, I don't think I've ever been rejected, not even in high school."

"Then you're one of the lucky ones," Nick said wryly. "Take it from me, rejection stinks."

Luke knew the faraway look on his brother's face meant he was remembering his long-ago secret marriage and subsequent rejection that had kept him from making a commitment to Abby. Eventually they had worked things out, thanks to Ma.

"Yeah," Luke said. "But the truth is, I never cared about being turned down. I can't help wondering if I'm incapable of falling in love. Except—"

"Go on."

"The last time I saw Maddie, I think I pushed her over the edge. She was different, even though she told me when her next appointment was and that I could be there if I chose. But when she walked away, I got this sinking feeling in my gut."

"It's called *scared to death*," Nick explained. "Guys aren't supposed to admit to it, because it goes against the unwritten code. But *scared* pretty much describes that gut feeling. And I think a pretty good indication that Maddie is 'the one,' as Mom would say."

"I wish I were as sure. I don't think falling in love is in the cards for me. Maybe it's the DNA from my biological father."

"Too bad you can't talk to him," Nick commented.

"Yeah. Although Maddie said I need to get over that."

"She's right. You should hang on to her. Still, it would probably help if you had a clue about the guy."

"He left me a letter. Maddie gave it to me when she handled the will. But I haven't read it yet," Luke admitted.

"Then I suggest you do." Nick stood. "But not on company time. Look, I was going to suggest you start tomorrow, but I'd really like you to look at the quarterlies. Would you mind? You're so much better at interpreting the numbers. Then we can go to lunch, I'll even buy."

Luke looked at his watch. "Maddie's appointment is at one. Can I take a rain check—"

"On lunch? Sure. I wouldn't press about work, but it's important. As a matter of fact, if you hadn't stopped by, I was going to call you and guilt you into coming in. Just get up to speed, then take off. Besides, the doctor always runs late. Abby practically reads a book every time she goes in for an appointment."

"Yeah. Okay," Luke said.

"It's good to have you back, Bro." Nick came around the desk and held out his hand.

Luke took it, then pulled his brother into a bear hug. "It's good to be back."

Luke missed Maddie at the doctor. For the first time in recorded history, Dr. Virginia Olsen had been running early. He had called Maddie's office, but the receptionist said she'd left early and they didn't expect her back for the rest of the day. He'd tried her at the condo, by phone and in person. If she was there, she wasn't picking up or answering the door. Either way, his foul mood didn't improve.

He paced his condo like a caged tiger, then finally went to the kitchen, where he'd put the letter. Since it wasn't likely to make his mood any worse, he decided it was high time he looked at the one and only clue he had about who his biological father was.

He easily found the wrinkled envelope with his name scrawled in the unfamiliar handwriting. Ripping it open, he left the envelope torn nearly in half and held two sheets of paper in trembling hands. How could this possibly tell him anything useful about the man?

"Here goes nothing," he said.

Dear Luke:

If you're reading this, it means I'm gone and you know the contents of my will. First, please accept my apologies. Your life has no doubt been turned upside down, and for that I'm deeply and profoundly sorry. But there's one thing I can never be sorry about—my relationship with your mother.

Until Flo, I'd never been in love. I'd begun to think there was something wrong with me, that I was incapable of deep feelings for any woman. I found out I couldn't have been more wrong. Unfortunately, the woman I fell for was married and very much in love with another man—an ambitious, busy man.

Luke, don't blame your mother for what happened. It's all my fault. I used her loneliness and vulnerability to get what I wanted. I'm not proud of it; I just need for you to understand. Flo, being who she is, told Tom everything. He forgave her, and I don't think it's too much to ask that you do the same.

We agreed to keep it a secret. I wanted to be a part of your life, but Flo and Tom convinced me that it would be best for you if I kept quiet and you didn't know the truth. Over time, as you grew into a fine, bright man, I came to see that they were right. But never, ever mistake my silence for lack of emotion. It doesn't mean that I never loved you. Just the opposite.

The last thing I'm sorry for is my selfishness. When I found out about the cancer, I couldn't bear ceasing to exist with no one to miss me. No one to think about me. No one to whom my very existence might have mattered. And on a practical note, no one to leave everything I'd spent my life working for.

Because your mother was the only woman I ever loved, I never married or had any other children. I'm a one-woman man.

I would give anything to have spared you the pain of knowing this, Luke. I regret that I wasn't a stronger man. But my biggest regret is that I never had the opportunity to be a father to you. To help you. My son. I wish you life's every happiness. I love you more than you'll ever know.

                                        Brad Stephenson

"Wow. So much for nothing." Luke let out a long breath and looked at the letter he'd just read. It explained so much. "You helped more than you'll ever know. I just hope it's not too late."

Chapter Twelve

Madison walked wearily into the condo and dropped her briefcase in the family room. From where she stood she could see the red light on her answering machine blinking, indicating there was a message.

Luke, she thought hopefully. No. Even if it was him, she wouldn't let it matter. She was never speaking to him again.

But that didn't mean she couldn't listen to him, just to hear his voice. She walked over to the machine and pushed the button. "Madison, it's Mother. Your father rearranged his schedule, and we will be able to come for a visit sooner. Call when you can. We both send best wishes, dear."

She suppressed her disappointment at not hearing the deep, wonderful tone of his voice. But she was glad her mother had called. Now that they'd started talking, she found her parents to be different, receptive, if still a bit reserved. But there was time to work on that, as well as get rid of her own resentment. They were the only parents she had, and her child's grandparents. It would be tragic to let old wounds keep her from having a relationship with them. She was looking forward to it.

And she had to admit that she had Luke to thank for it. But she would only admit it to herself. After all, she was never speaking to Luke Marchetti again.

Her doorbell rang. It was him. It had to be. Her instant reaction was unbridled joy. Then common sense crept in and she remembered she wasn't talking to him. Briefly she toyed with the idea of not answering, pretending she wasn't home. But her lights were on, and she knew how persistent he was. After all, he'd asked her to marry him three times. She'd turned him down all three. And, darn it all, he'd finally gotten the message. Technically, he'd gotten the wrong message, which was that she didn't want to marry him.

She wanted to, very much. But only if he wanted her for the right reason. She sighed. After yesterday, that wasn't likely to happen. He'd sent her a message, too, by his absence at the doctor. That had spoken volumes.

The doorbell rang again, and she huffed, "Oh, all right. I'm coming."

She opened the door. Instead of Luke, a flower arrangement was standing on her doorstep. Or rather, a neighbor from the condo complex was standing there with the flowers. "Mrs. Galloway."

"Hi, Madison. These were delivered for you, and I agreed to keep them. Who's Luke?"

"There was a card without an envelope?"

"Sticking right out on that plastic fork thing smack-dab in the center."

And she was the queen of Sheba, Madison thought. But what did it matter if her nosy neighbor knew the sender's name. She still wasn't speaking to him. Although the red roses, two dozen unless she missed her guess, were very lovely. "Luke is a client of mine."

The diminutive, fiftyish blond woman winked as she handed her the huge arrangement. "Maybe. But this says he wants to be more."

"Thank you, Mrs. Galloway. I appreciate your taking care of them for me."

"Don't forget to invite me to the wedding. Good night, dear."

"Right. Good night," Madison said, closing the door.

As the fragrance of the flowers filled the room, tears sprang to her eyes. "Damn hormones," she grumbled, blinking rapidly. "Damn a wedding. And damn Luke."

She walked into the kitchen and set them on the table. "What is he trying to do? Drive me crazy, that's what."

The doorbell rang again. "That's probably Mrs. Galloway with the missing envelope," she said to herself.

She walked through the living room and opened the door. "It wasn't necessary to— Luke!"

He stood there with his fingertips in the pockets of his navy slacks, leaning against the wall. What a delicious sight for her sore eyes. The sleeves of his white, long-sleeved shirt were rolled to the elbow, and his red silk tie was loose at the neck. Her traitorous heart pounded at the lovely sight of him. Just because she enjoyed look-ing—drank in the sight of his sensuous mouth, delighted in his dynamite dimples, worried at the weary lines around his eyes—didn't mean she had anything to say to him. His name just popped out because she was sur-prised to see him.

"May I come in? I don't think you want your neigh-bors to eavesdrop on what I have to say. In fact, I just passed a small, blond woman who wanted to know if I was Luke."

Madison shrugged, stepped back and held her hand out to admit him inside.

"Can we sit down?" he asked, starting for the kitchen. It was a moment or two before he realized she wasn't behind him. He stopped and lifted a questioning brow.

She held out her hand to indicate they should sit in the living room. After all, the family room was for family. He would never be part of hers. Her heart broke at the thought. Keep it formal, she warned. The living room was the best place to do that.

He lowered his tall, muscular frame to her plush sofa, looking masculine enough to die for in her feminine surroundings. Sitting with his legs spread wide and his elbows resting on his knees, fingers intertwined, he appeared ill at ease. Good. He had a lot to be ill at ease about, she decided.

He looked at her and waited. Finally he said, "I don't need divine intervention from the burning bush to get that you're not speaking to me."

She shrugged and met his gaze, letting her chin go up just a fraction.

He nodded. "That's okay. I just need you to listen. Although it does seem a contradiction in terms for an attorney to keep her mouth shut."

Her only answer was to sit on the matching love seat and demurely fold her hands in her lap. Why should she believe that he had anything different to say? Anything of importance that she would want to hear?

"I talked to my folks."

He'd called them? He'd fulfilled his part of their bargain?

He looked at his hands, then met her gaze. "Actually I went to see them. Everything everyone has been trying to make me see has finally sunk in. It was right there in front of me and I didn't get it.''

She wanted to ask what it was, but she just shifted her position and uncrossed her legs.

"It was the biggest clue of all," he continued. "I never suspected that I was different."

"Huh?"

He grinned, a fleeting smile that tugged at her heart. "I knew you couldn't do it for long."

"It's just my legal training kicking in. Nothing more," she said.

"Whatever you say. Anyway, the fact that I wasn't treated specially or differently in any way from my siblings means that I am Tom Marchetti's son."

"Well it's about darn time," she said. "The bigger they are, the more stubborn, and the harder they fall."

"You won't get any argument from me about that." He stuck his hands in his pockets. "I wanted you to know, too, that I went back to work at Marchetti's."

"I figured that. The slacks and tie were a clue."

"I took your advice. I'm keeping the business Brad Stephenson left me. I have someone in mind to run it. I've already talked with him about instituting a job-training program through the women's shelter you've been working with."

She leaned forward eagerly. "What a wonderful idea, Luke. Housing only solves a temporary problem. It's like a Band-Aid on a Buick-size breach in the levee. They need jobs to support themselves and their children."

The corners of his mouth turned up, causing her pulse to skip. "Has anyone ever mentioned that you have a way with words, Counselor?"

"They're my life."

"I hope not entirely, because I have a lot more to say. A confession, actually."

Here it comes. He can't love me, she thought. She didn't want to hear him say it. "For a man of numbers, I think you've probably used up your quota of words."

"I've hardly begun." He cleared his throat. "All of my adult life I thought one woman was pretty much like another. No one touched me in any special way. My history with women was one fling after another, without any emotional engagement."

"I see," was all she could manage to say before emotion closed her throat and made her catch her top lip between her teeth to keep from crying out.

"No, you don't see. I just got it."

"What happened? Did Tom say something?"

He shook his head. "I finally read the letter."

She gasped and started to reach out to him before she caught herself and curled her fingers into her palm. "Oh, Luke. Are you all right?"

"Yeah. It's like the light went on," he said. "I've been pretty confused."

"Oh?"

A twinkle momentarily appeared in his eyes at her noncommittal understatement, then disappeared as he turned serious again. "The night of Alex's wedding, when I kissed you, something happened. Something was different. Then we made love and I discovered you were a virgin."

"Yes," she said blushing. "But we don't have to go through that again. Can't we just forget—"

"No, Maddie. I won't ever forget it. It's the most precious gift I've ever received. And it scared the bejeezus out of me."

"But why?"

"The kiss was special. But I was still thinking fling. Until I found out you'd never given yourself to another man. Until me. That implied commitment. I had a track record of no harm, no foul, no obligation. But you're different—special."

A tiny seed of hope blossomed in her heart. "What are you trying to say, Luke?"

"After all these years it had never happened to me. I didn't think I was capable of caring about anyone enough to make a life with them. I thought there was something wrong with me."

"And?" she asked breathlessly.

"I found out why. I take after my biological father. Good and bad."

"How so?"

"You were right about me. I don't like losing and I'll do what it takes to win. Although you think of it as getting my way."

She permitted herself a small smile. "I believe I said you were acting like a child."

"And you were right. And I plan to work on that. But the point is Brad was like that, too. He wanted my mother. He fell in love with her and saw her vulnerability when my father was building the restaurant chain. He caught her at a time when she was feeling unloved, unattractive and coming unglued with three small boys to take care of with little support. He flattered her and gave her what she needed at the time."

"Oh, Luke."

"It's okay. I finally understand. Ma and I are okay. Tom—Dad—forgave her years ago. How could I not? The three of them agreed that I should be raised with the rest of the family, no different from the others. Brad trusted me to Tom and I was never the wiser. Because he was a good father. And he loved me.''

"It was a courageous decision for Brad.''

Luke nodded. ''I know that now. But his letter was a gift. He gave me the piece of myself that no one else could.''

"What's that?''

"He never married or had any other children. That was part of why he broke his promise to keep the secret. He wanted to leave me the business he'd worked all his life for. But he only ever loved my mother. He was a one-woman man. And I'm exactly like him.''

Hope grew in her chest like combustible gas in a hot-air balloon. ''I'm glad you understand better now.''

"I need to apologize to you, Maddie. I did try to control you. I'm not proud of it. But at least now I understand.''

"What do you understand?''

He stood up and started pacing. ''When you turned me down, my life stretched before me like a black hole, without light or color. Each time I asked and you turned me down, I grew more desperate. More pushy and underhanded. But I have a good reason. I love you.''

Her heart was so full, she could hardly stand it. But she had some things to say, as well. ''I have a confession to make, too,'' she said.

"What could you possibly have to tell me?''

"I need to thank you for giving me a chance with my family. If it hadn't been for you, for your belief in me, your insistence that I was the only person who could help you, that I *mattered,* I never would have had the guts to make that call to my parents. You gave me a precious gift, too. My self-esteem.''

"You're a bright, beautiful, funny, lovable woman. Sooner or later you would have figured that out."

"I'm not so sure. But the point is I'm talking to my parents. In fact they've offered me a place to live, with the baby. No questions asked."

His face fell. "I don't know what to say. Are you going to take them up on it? What about your job? You've worked really hard for a partnership. You wouldn't chuck it all now."

"Sure I would. There are some things more important than power and prestige. Family."

"I see." He rubbed the back of his neck. "I guess we can work something out. Other people do long-distance parenting. It was dumb to think you would need me as much as I need—"

"Me?" she asked, tears filling her eyes. "Do you really need me, want me?"

He took a step toward her and stopped in front of her. Reaching down he took her hands in his and pulled her to her feet. Squeezing gently he said, "Lady, I need you more than my next breath. More than I need water to drink or food to eat. You are my sunlight and my every happiness. I want you. I need you. And I will swear this on a stack of Bibles if it will satisfy your sense of jurisprudence—I have always wanted children. I want our baby more than I can say." Still holding her hands, he went down on one knee. "Marry me, Maddie. Let's make a family together. Don't leave me."

"I never said I was going to accept my parents' offer. Just that it was more important than a job."

"Then I have a chance. Do you love me?" he asked.

"Love you? I think the sun rises and sets on you. I love you more than my life," she said. "Yes, I'll marry you. Nothing would make me happier than being your wife and having your child.''

His mouth curved into a wide, oh-so-attractive grin. ''Fourth time is the charm.''

''But who's counting?'' she said, slipping into his arms, the only place on earth she wanted to be.

''I am. Numbers are my thing. I intend to count the next fifty years with you.''

She laughed, and the sound was filled with happiness. ''Do you remember when I made that foolish vow to never get involved with another Marchetti man?''

He nodded. ''And you kept it. Technically I'm not a Marchetti.''

Thankfully he made the statement without any shadows clouding his expression. She was so happy. ''No, you're not. But you're luckier than most. You have two wonderful fathers. And, in my humble opinion, the last Marchetti bachelor is definitely the best man.''

''My Maddie.''

''I think I've always been your Maddie.''

He kissed her soundly. ''I'll spend the rest of my life doing everything possible to make sure you never change your mind about that.''

Epilogue

Five years later

From a dais set up in the center of the banquet room, Luke and Maddie along with his siblings and their spouses surveyed the first Marchetti's restaurant that his father had ever opened. It was full of family and friends helping to celebrate his parents' fortieth wedding anniversary. Nick and Abby stood at the podium to make a toast.

"Where do I begin?" Nick put his arm around pregnant Abby and drew her closer to his side. "Mom and Dad have accomplished a lot in forty years. A successful restaurant chain. I hope I've done them proud, since I've been at the company helm. We've just opened the first restaurant on the east coast," he added. "But Mom and Dad's highest priority is and always has been family."

Abby took the microphone he handed her. Her blond hair shimmered in a pageboy around her face as her sky-blue eyes looked adoringly at her husband. "I fell in love with Nick the day he gave me a job at Marchetti's when I was an eighteen-year-old kid who had just lost her parents and was raising a little sister. Sarah's grown up now and has one more year at UCLA where she will earn her degree, then go on to teach. Her fiancé Austin Reese is pre-med and has been accepted into medical school there." She put a hand on her rounded tummy. "Nick and I are working on baby number three." She glanced up at her husband and said, "I have inside information that it's another girl. Sorry, honey."

Nick leaned over to the microphone. "Thank heaven for little girls," he said. There was loud laughter and applause.

Abby laughed. "I job share the manager's position in one of the Marchetti restaurants with another working mother." She looked over at Tom and Flo who were sitting side by side. "Mom and Dad, here's to you. Thanks for everything." She held out the microphone.

Joe took it in one hand and held his wife, Liz, with his other. "That goes for us, too. If not for you, I wouldn't have this wonderful woman by my side. I met her through the cuddler's program when I was searching for what was missing in my life. The commitment you two gave to your relationship convinced her to take a chance on me. And now we have two boys and a girl to cuddle."

Liz took the microphone from him as he put a hand on her gently rounded belly. "And another on the way. I've got a feeling it's a boy."

Joe leaned over and said into the mike, "Never underestimate the ESP of a pregnant lady."

Liz laughed. "With my wonderful husband's blessing and support, I've retired as a nurse, for now at least, to raise our children. But Joe and I volunteer in the hospital's cuddler's program every chance we get. And I still moderate a class for new moms. With job training under my belt, so to speak, I think I can finally do it justice." She looked at Flo and Tom. "Without you and the wonderful son you raised, all of this happiness wouldn't have been possible. Thank you," she said, her voice breaking.

Alex stepped beside her and took the mike. He held his wife, Fran's, hand. "I'm in charge of marketing as well as research and development for the company my father founded. Frannie and I created a successful line of frozen foods that's kicking butt in that market. But more important, it's how we met. I had the good sense to hire her and then marry her. We have a beautiful little boy," he said, then caressed her gently protruding stomach. "And another on the way."

Fran took the mike. "Since my sisters-in-law are going on record publicly, I will, too. Based on the fact that there are four boys in Alex's family and four in mine, I think the odds are good that this baby is a boy, too."

Alex smiled broadly. "Thank heaven for little boys. And we'll just have to keep trying till we get a girl."

"No matter how many it takes?" Fran asked. She laughed when he nodded. "Thanks to my wonderful husband and his family, this last year I achieved my lifelong dream of opening a restaurant of my own. His only stipulation was that it be American food and not competition for Marchetti's. It's a small, quiet place in West Los Angeles. Thanks to a positive write-up in the *L.A. Times,* and great word of mouth, we're really catching on. Thanks Mom and Dad Marchetti, for this fabulous guy. He had the best examples in the world." She placed her hand protectively on her stomach. "Now I can slow down and concentrate on our family. We have to catch up with Alex's sister, Rosie, and her husband, Steve."

Never letting go of her husband's hand, curly haired, brown-eyed, petite Rosie took the mike. "Mom and Dad, I have you to thank for Steve, the love of my life. Your devotion to children didn't end with your own. You took a mixed-up boy under your wing, and he grew into a terrific man. He's the best husband and father I could ever have asked for. And a pretty good businessman, too. He does security background checks for some of the largest companies in the country."

Steve put his hand over hers and brought the mike up to his mouth. "Thanks, Mom and Dad, for this woman. I'd be a mess without her. Now that she's pregnant with baby number five, I talked her into hiring a manager for her thriving bookstore. We found the ideal employee the same way Abby found the right person to share the restaurant manager's position. But we'll let Luke and Maddie tell you about that."

Luke took the microphone. "Rosie, any guess on what the baby is?"

She leaned over. "We have girl, boy, girl, boy. I'm guessing this little one is a boy. And I wouldn't bet against me. I've been right every time."

Luke put his arm around Maddie's expanding waist and pulled her against him. "I wouldn't be here tonight or be the man I am without you, Mom and Dad. I'm the CFO at Marchetti's," he added.

His wife put her hand over his and tugged the microphone close to her mouth. "And I'm Maddie, Mrs. CFO. Thanks to him, and his genius with finances, not one of us would ever have to work again if we didn't want to. He's too modest to say that."

Luke laughed. "On top of singing my praises, my wife handles legal work from my accounting franchise, in between taking care of our three children. And another on the way," he said proudly. "Care to take a guess what it is, sweetheart?"

She leaned over. "We've got Lucy, Thomas Bradley and Winifred. I'm guessing this baby is a boy. We've got to maintain gender balance," she said, producing a laugh and a round of applause from the audience.

"She's never been wrong, either," Luke said. "But besides family, something near and dear to our hearts is Haven House, the women's shelter my wife champions. Maddie was determined to do something worthwhile, and she has. She's helped numerous women get back on their feet and rebuild their lives through training programs and job placement. I'm humbled, but profoundly grateful that she agreed to marry me and share my life."

He walked over to where his parents were sitting and kissed his mother's cheek, then shook his father's hand and embraced him. He lifted the cracked and patched crystal bowl filled with flowers that sat in the center of their table.

"This is very precious to all of us. It's a symbol of my parent's commitment and determination that their family would flourish." He set it back down. "From the bottom of my heart, I thank you both for everything I am and everything I have."

Thundering applause followed, then the DJ played music for dancing. Luke pulled Maddie into his embrace, and they weren't as concerned about the steps as they were just holding each other.

"So Mrs. Marchetti," he said. "Do you think we should rescue your mom and dad from Lucy, Tommy and Winnie?"

Maddie glanced over her shoulder to where Grandpa and Grammy looked to be having the time of their lives doing the hokey-pokey with their grandchildren ages five, four and two and a half. She met his gaze, and he saw the twinkle of mischief in her own. Together they said, "Nah."

"It keeps them from reverting to their stuffiness," she said. "They've learned to open up and lighten up. Grandkids are the best thing that ever happened to them."

"You're the best thing that ever happened to me," he said.

"I could say the same about you." She gazed up at him with love shining in her eyes. "I can hardly remember the time before I was surrounded by a large, loving family."

"I promise to do everything within my power to keep that particular expression on your beautiful, freckled face for the rest of your life."

"Just be you," she said simply.

"If good genes and a positive environment can turn a mutt like me into—"

"The best man," she finished for him.

"If you say so. But I'm living proof that love makes anything possible."

If he was the best man, it was because he'd learned from the best—his parents. Correction—all of his parents. And he could never thank them enough.

* * * * *

Spines will tingle…mysteries await…
and dangerous passion lurks in the night
as Silhouette presents

DREAM SCAPES!

Thrills and chills abound in these four romances
welcoming readers to the dark side of love.
Available May 2001 at your favorite retail outlet:

IMMINENT THUNDER
by Rachel Lee

STRANGER IN THE MIST
by Lee Karr

FLASHBACK
by Terri Herrington

NOW AND FOREVER
by Kimberly Raye

Silhouette
bestselling authors

KASEY
MICHAELS

RUTH
LANGAN

CAROLYN
ZANE

*welcome you to a world
of family, privilege and power
with three brand-new love
stories about America's
most beloved dynasty,
the Coltons*

*Brides
of
Privilege*

Available May 2001

Silhouette
Where love comes alive™

Visit Silhouette at www.eHarlequin.com
PSCOLT

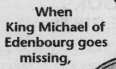